PLACE YOUR TRUST IN ME

SEASONED ROMANCE SERIES

BOOK THREE

ELIZABETH KELLY

EK PUBLISHING INC.

Published by:
EK Publishing Inc.

ISBN: 978-1-77446-166-2

Edited by:
L. Nunn Editing

Cover art by
EK Designs

PLACE YOUR TRUST IN ME

Judge Sierra Walters has one goal—to prove her ex-husband wrong.

After years of making her ex's dreams her priority, Sierra is determined to focus on her needs for the first time. Which includes restoring the fixer-upper she's living in, no matter how many DIY videos she must watch or how many weekends she has to give up.

Except drywalling is her downfall.

She's forced to hire contractor Everett Caine to get the job done. She isn't expecting Everett to be so funny or have a delightfully hard body she aches to explore... with her tongue.

Soured toward commitment, at fifty-six Everett Caine is happy and single. Perfect for concentrating on his business.

He knows better than to get involved with a client. It's messy. It's complicated. And never ends well. Yet, it only takes one glance, and he suddenly can't stop imagining Sierra draped across his bed. The woman pokes and prods every one of his buttons, whether it's using her beautiful mouth to tell him off or to turn him on.

But as the intense attraction grows between them, will Sierra and Everett realize that achieving their dreams is easier done together? Or will they let past hurts and old wounds split them apart?

CHAPTER 1

S ierra would rather be stung in the ass by a thousand bees than talk to her ex-husband.

Unfortunately, despite the warm spring weather, no bees hovered around her driveway, ready to give her an excuse not to answer her phone. She sighed and slid behind the wheel of her car, ignoring her steadily buzzing phone as she started the vehicle.

Her phone stopped vibrating and then started again only thirty seconds later. The screen on her dashboard showed that Spawn of Satan was calling.

She backed out of the driveway and considered continuing to ignore Gary before hitting the answer button on the steering wheel. She'd been married to the man for years. She knew better than anyone how stubborn he could be.

"Hello, Gary." She kept her voice pleasant and didn't let any of her annoyance bleed through.

Gary didn't return the favour nor bother with pleasantries. "We need to talk about the house."

"Whose house?" She drove down her street, waving at her

neighbour, Mrs. Dennison, who was planting annuals in her front flower bed.

Gary's impatient sigh echoed in the car interior. "Your house."

"Why?" she asked.

"Why?" He parroted like it was the stupidest question in the world. "Because that piece of shit fixer-upper is affecting our daughter's future, Sierra."

Since the divorce, Gary couldn't say her name without sounding like he wanted to dip her in acid.

"What are you talking about, Gary?" It was getting harder and harder to keep her tone civil.

"I'm talking about the amount of money you're sinking into that money pit," Gary said. "Do you even have enough to cover Michaela's university costs?"

"In case you've forgotten, we're not married anymore. My money and what I do with it is none of your business," Sierra said.

"Of course it is!" Gary snapped. "I don't want our daughter quitting university because her mother can't help share tuition costs like she promised."

"I'm not reneging on my promise." Sierra's voice turned icy. "I am more than capable of paying my share of Michaela's tuition."

"I don't see how," Gary said. "Michaela told me how much money you're spending on the house. I told you buying a fixer-upper was a mistake, but you wouldn't listen because no one tells Sierra Lewis what to do, isn't that right? Your stubbornness and refusal to let me give you a single helpful suggestion is ending Michaela's education just like it ended our marriage."

She didn't rise to the bait. What was the point? He believed she was to blame for the end of their marriage, and nothing she said would ever change that. His absolute refusal to accept blame for their marital issues was nothing new.

"I've already paid my portion of Michaela's tuition for this semester," Sierra said as she merged onto the main highway in their small town. "You're on my ass about nothing, Gary."

"I'm on your ass?" Gary said. "Oh, that's rich coming from the woman who rode my ass about my mistakes every goddamn day of our marriage."

"I'm hanging up now, Gary," she said.

"I know you hired a drywaller," he said quickly. "Michaela told me."

"So, what?" The change in topic made her head spin.

"You said you were doing the renovations yourself."

She pulled into a parking space at Home Depot. "I am, but drywall isn't something an average person can do."

"You said you would do it all yourself. That's what you said to me, Sierra. But I guess it's just another promise you've broken, huh?"

"I'm going to say this one last time, Gary. How I live my life is none of your business." Sierra was so angry she could hardly get the words out.

"I'm just trying to help, Sierra," Gary said.

She pushed the end call button on her steering wheel and shut off the car. Her phone started to vibrate, and she shoved it deep into her purse and gripped the steering wheel.

"Ignore him, Sierra," she told her reflection in the rearview mirror. "Don't let him get under your skin."

Easier said than done. Gary knew all the spots to poke and prod, and sometimes, she felt helpless against the assault. She couldn't say what she really wanted to say to him, not if she didn't want to strain her relationship with Michaela.

For all his faults, Gary was a fantastic dad, and he and

Michaela had a close relationship. Sierra was happy about that, she really was, but it did mean biting her tongue a lot. She'd promised Michaela they would always be a family and kept that promise since the divorce. No matter how hard Gary made it.

And Jesus, sometimes he made it so fucking hard.

Sierra had hoped that when Gary remarried a few years ago, it might ease his bitterness toward her over leaving him. It was clear how much Gary loved Roxanne and how much she loved him, but even with his new wife, he wouldn't let go of his anger toward Sierra for ending their marriage.

She took a deep breath, grabbed her purse, and climbed out of the car. She didn't want Gary's words to upset her, but she was angry, frustrated, and completely over the fact that even six years after their divorce, he still thought he could tell her what to do.

She walked into Home Depot. She'd been here so much in the last couple of years that she was confident she could walk the entire store blindfolded and find precisely what she was looking for.

The store was busy for a Friday morning, and she might have been angry over her conversation with her ex-husband, but she still noticed the guy standing in aisle fourteen.

She was angry, not dead.

She slowed her step, pretending to study the packages of sandpaper on the end cap but, in reality, drinking in the delicious cool glass of water texting on his phone.

He was in his mid to late fifties with short silver hair and a matching silver beard cropped close to his jaw. He wore a plain blue t-shirt with a grey and white plaid shirt layered over it and a pair of jeans that hung low on his hips. She studied his hands. They were big and rough looking. A man

4

who did manual labour, she decided, as muscles low in her belly twinged.

Maybe he was a lumberjack. He certainly had the upper body for it, and she could easily picture him swinging an axe in the middle of the forest. Maybe without the plaid shirt, though. Plaid wasn't her thing.

But damn, he made her want to change her mind about her no-plaid stance. A man who looked like him could wear whatever the hell he wanted, as long as she got to strip it off of him later.

Her lumberjack fantasy was getting a little too hot and heavy for aisle fourteen of Home Depot. Imagining how those big, rough hands would feel against her naked ass was definitely a bad idea. Especially since he wasn't even glancing her way, and... she took a second look at his left hand, yup, that was a wedding band.

She sighed and walked past him. He didn't look up, and she didn't bother taking a second look at the lumberjack of her dreams. She didn't flirt, fantasize, or fuck with married men.

She stopped in front of the wall anchors, looking over the options. An employee entered the aisle and gave Sierra a friendly smile. "Hi, I'm Melissa. Is there something I can help you with today?"

"I'm hanging a shelf in my kitchen to display my cookbooks," Sierra said. "I'm looking at drywall anchor options."

"Ah, okay. You'll want these here." Melissa reached out and snagged a plastic package from one of the pegs. "A threaded wall anchor will work for you."

"Fantastic, thanks." Sierra took the anchors from her.

"You're welcome. Have a great day!" Melissa chirped before leaving.

Sierra studied the anchors she held, but before she could

follow Melissa out of the aisle, a - *sweet Jesus* - ridiculously deep and sexy voice said, "Excuse me?"

She turned to see Mr. Lumberjack himself standing behind her. Fuck, he smelled great, and now that she was this close to him, it was impossible not to notice his straight white teeth or pretty hazel eyes.

Off limits, Sierra!

Right. Sexy Lumberjack Man was married. She smiled at him, but not with her *you want to fuck me* smile. "Hello."

"Hi," he said. "Just an FYI, if you're putting cookbooks on that shelf, the threaded wall anchor won't work."

She glanced at the package she held, her attraction to the man dying an immediate death. It didn't matter how pretty he was or how good he smelled, she was over men assuming she was utterly helpless. As it often did, her sarcasm leaped into the light. "Huh, and here I was thinking you were a lumberjack."

"Sorry?" His look of confusion would have been adorable if she hadn't been so annoyed.

She pointed to his shirt. "I thought you were a lumber-jack, not a Home Depot employee."

"I think they're called loggers now, and I'm not one, nor do I work here," he said.

"So, you're commenting on my wall anchors because why?" she said.

"Because the associate who helped you has her informa-tion wrong."

"Why? Because she's a woman?" Sierra asked.

His confusion turned to an amusement that just pissed her off more. "No, not everything is about man versus woman."

"Ah, the audacity of the mediocre white man. You don't think that's true because you don't have to. No one's coming up to you and telling you you're wrong," she said.

Exasperation mixed with the amusement. "This isn't me being sexist. This is me telling you that you need a toggle anchor or a molly bolt so that -"

"Thank you, but I don't need your mansplaining," she said.

"Jesus, it's not about that," he said. "I'm trying to help."

How many fucking times had Gary said that to her throughout their marriage? Too many to count, and their most recent conversation only proved that he would always fucking do it. Obviously, it was a guy thing and not just a Gary thing, but she was one hundred percent fucking over it. And even though she knew she was taking out her frustration and her annoyance with her ex-husband on Mr. Sexy Lumberjack, she couldn't seem just to let it the fuck go.

"But I didn't ask for your help, did I?" She fixed him with her best judge look. The one that made the criminals in her courtroom second guess their belief that she would go easy on them because she was a woman.

The man studied her. He wasn't intimidated - she had a feeling it took a lot more than a look to intimidate him - but he held up his hands in a no offense gesture and stepped back. "You're right. My bad. Have a great day, ma'am."

He turned and walked away. She refrained from staring at his ass and yelling at him not to call her ma'am. Both were pointless actions.

Her cheeks hot and her stomach in a tight knot, she turned and walked in the opposite direction.

CHAPTER 2

"It looks great. Nice job, Sierra," Hazel said.

"Thank you." Sierra flipped the camera on her phone, and Hazel's smiling face appeared on the screen. "And thank you for taking time away from your shop to admire my new cookbook shelf."

Hazel laughed. "You're welcome. Although it's weirdly quiet in the shop this morning, and Ruby has already made all the custom bouquets for today, so I will admit it was easy to sneak away for a video chat."

"Being the owner probably helps with the sneaking away, too," Sierra said.

"True," Hazel said. "Hey, did you meet with Hendrix's drywaller friend yet? I thought Hendrix said it was this week."

"Today, actually." Sierra sank into a kitchen chair and sipped at her tea. "It's why I took the day off. Everett could only meet this afternoon."

"What time is he stopping by?" Hazel asked. She was in the back room of her flower shop, and Sierra could see a shelf piled high with flower foam and tissue paper behind Hazel.

"Any time now," Sierra said. "He was supposed to be here at two, but he texted that he was finishing up a job at a client's and would be a little late."

"Cool. Let me know how it goes. Oh, are you still coming to Indie's tonight for dinner?" Hazel asked.

"Yep," Sierra said. "Can you text me Val's address? I haven't been to his place yet."

"Seriously? Indie moved in with him a month ago," Hazel said.

"I know. I'm a bad friend."

Hazel frowned. "No, you're not. I didn't mean it that way."

"I know. I just… I feel like a bad friend. The renovations are sucking up all of my spare time, and I'm neglecting you and Indie."

"You absolutely are not," Hazel said. "Just because you missed the last two Wednesday night dinners doesn't mean you're neglecting us. It just means you're busy, and we understand."

"I really wanted to get the bathroom gutted before the drywaller inspects the walls," Sierra said. "I'm hoping that the walls can be patched rather than replaced, but I'm not holding my breath. There are pretty significant water stains on two of the walls."

"I'll keep my fingers crossed for you," Hazel said.

"Thanks. I'm also hoping Everett can work fast. I'm tired of having a soaker tub in my bedroom."

Hazel laughed. "I'm not sure that working fast is a thing any contractor does, but Hendrix has nothing but good things to say about this Everett guy. They go for beers usually once a week or so."

"Have you met him?" Sierra asked.

"Just once, very briefly," Hazel said. "He was

friendly, a little on the quiet side. Also, he was hot as hell."

"Hey, is an engaged woman supposed to be checking out other men?" Sierra said teasingly.

"What's that saying? I may be on a diet, but I can still look at the menu," Hazel said.

Sierra laughed. "Fair. Hey, I better run. I think I heard a car door slam."

"Okay, good luck with Everett, the hot drywaller. I'll see you tonight!" Hazel ended the call.

The doorbell rang, and Sierra left the kitchen and quickly checked her makeup in the hallway mirror. Not that she was planning on banging the hot drywaller, but she also didn't want to look like a complete hag.

She smoothed her t-shirt and her hair before opening the door. The welcoming smile on her face faded as she stared at the man standing on her front porch.

She sighed. "Well, shit."

EVERETT SLAMMED HIS TRUCK DOOR AND WALKED UP THE driveway to the craftsman style home. He took a moment to admire the house. Craftsman homes were his personal favourite, and this one, while a little rough looking in some parts, had great potential.

The outside had peeling brown paint, and the square tapered columns supporting the covered front porch needed a fresh coat of white paint. But the roof was brand new, and the front door was a warm cherry wood with three decorative opaque glass panels along the top and a design of two wooden panels underneath.

The house would look great if painted a warm mossy

green colour, and some landscaping was added around the porch, he mused.

He climbed the porch steps and rang the doorbell. The porch floor was freshly stained, and he grinned at the welcome mat that said "Welcome-ish (depends who you are)" in bold black letters.

His gaze caught a glimmer of gold, and he studied the fake wedding band on his left hand. He'd forgotten to take the damn thing off after finishing at Selma Ratkin's place.

He reached for the ring as the door opened. He glanced up, the smile on his face dropping away. The sexy as fuck woman from Home Depot this morning, the one who'd managed to both irritate and turn him on, stood in the doorway.

She sighed. "Well, shit."

He studied her pretty brown eyes and full mouth. The very mouth he'd spent an inappropriate amount of time earlier today envisioning wrapped around his dick.

It'd been almost thirty seconds, and he was still staring at her mouth. The back of his neck went hot. Christ, he could at least try to be professional.

"Ms. Lewis? I'm Everett Caine. It's nice to meet you formally." He held out his hand.

She stared at it for a few seconds before shaking his hand firmly. "It's nice to meet you, Mr. Caine. Please come in."

He stepped inside, slipping fabric booties over his shoes as she crossed her arms across her torso. Her face looked like she wanted to be anywhere but in her front hallway.

She cleared her throat. "So, listen, about earlier today, I -"

"I'm on a time limit today, Ms. Lewis, so if you don't mind, I'd like to start the bathroom inspection."

Her face flushed, and she nodded. "Of course. Follow me."

He was being a dick for no reason other than he was still annoyed by her mansplaining dig from earlier. Of course, his annoyance didn't stop him from checking out her spectacular ass clad in tight denim as he followed her up the stairs.

He guessed her age to be somewhere in her early forties, which made her a little too young for him, but damn, what he wouldn't give to see that spectacular ass of hers naked and across his lap. It would look beautiful covered in his handprints.

His palm itched, and he gave his dick a quick adjustment. He needed to stop thinking about spanking the gorgeous woman with the smart mouth before he had a full blown erection.

An erection would get him a terrible Yelp review.

He followed her down the hall to the last door on the right. She opened it, and he followed her into what he assumed was her bedroom. It was a large room with two windows lining one wall and a king-sized bed sandwiched between them. The bed was made, and the room was relatively tidy, but a free-standing white soaker tub took up a good chunk of space, and half a dozen boxes of laminate flooring were lined up in a row along the far wall.

"Ignore the tub," she said as she navigated around it. "It was delivered much earlier than expected."

"It's a nice tub," he said. "You got it at Badeloft?"

She gave him a look of surprise. "That's right. You know your tubs."

"You know us lumberjacks, we love a good soak after a long day," he said.

Her face flushed again, and he told himself to knock it off as he watched that pretty soft pink fill her high cheekbones.

"Right," she said, her voice stiff.

He pushed past the tub and followed her into the attached bathroom. "This is much bigger than I expected."

She nodded. "It's one of the reasons I bought this particular house - the large main bedroom and bathroom."

The bathroom had been completely gutted, with the flooring pulled up and pipes where the toilet, shower, and sink should have been.

"As you can see, there's some water damage along this wall here and over here," she said. "I knew about the damage on this wall, it was visible even with the vanity, but it wasn't until I was demoing the bathroom and removed the old tub/shower unit that I realized how extensive the water damage was along this wall."

"Who did you get to do the demolition?" he asked. He was impressed at how thorough and clean the demo was. He'd seen a lot of ugly demos where more damage had been done than necessary.

"I did it myself," she said.

"You did it yourself," he repeated.

She nodded, and he couldn't help it. His gaze drifted down her body. She was about average height and had a toned and strong-looking athletic body, but he still couldn't picture her gutting an entire bathroom.

She cleared her throat again, and he returned his gaze to her face. "Just because I'm a woman doesn't mean I'm incapable of gutting a bathroom, Mr. Caine."

"I didn't say you were," he countered. "But demoing a bathroom isn't usually a one-person job."

That pink flush deepened. "I did most of it myself," she amended, "with some help from friends for removing the bigger stuff like the vanity and tub."

He didn't reply, and she said, "You know one of them. Hendrix Smith."

"Hendrix is a good guy," he said.

"He is," she said. "I bought this house intending to do as much of the renovations myself as possible. But I quickly realized that drywalling wasn't something I could watch a DIY YouTube video on. Despite what the internet would have me believe."

He grinned. "Thanks to those DIY YouTube videos, a good chunk of my clients are people who tried to do the drywall themselves, and it went... badly. So very badly."

She laughed, and the sound went straight to his dick. "I believe that. Anyway, I'll get out of your hair and let you do your inspection. I'll be downstairs in the kitchen if you need me."

Her gaze dropped to his chest and upper arms before she brushed past him and left the room. He breathed deeply. Her lingering scent was light and floral and more appealing than he wanted it to be.

He shook his head to clear the cobwebs she created with just her presence. He was here to do a job, which did not include fantasizing about fucking the client. No matter how sexy he found her.

CHAPTER 3

"Okay, this is fine. Everything's fine." Sierra paced in her kitchen, glancing at the microwave clock and her phone. Did she have time to phone Hazel and have a mini freak out before Everett returned downstairs?

Probably not.

She sighed and leaned against the counter, staring out the window above the sink. She didn't even know why Everett had bothered to inspect the bathroom. After what happened at Home Depot, there was no way he'd take the job. Which meant she was back to square one. Trying to find a good reliable drywaller.

Fuck.

She just had to open her mouth at the store. Just had to let her conversation with Gary affect her to the point where she berated strangers at the fucking hardware store. She had no one but herself to blame.

Sure, but he did offer his advice when it wasn't needed.

Maybe, but had too many years of living with Gary soured her so much toward men? She hadn't thought so, but what happened today suggested it had.

Oh, please, you only regret what you said because Everett is hot as hell, and you want to fuck him.

He's married, she snapped.

That shut up her inner voice, thank fucking God.

Besides, even if he wasn't married, she couldn't fuck him. At least not until he'd finished the drywalling.

He's not taking the job.

Right. She needed to start calling drywallers again, and this time, she wouldn't benefit from Hendrix's help. She'd fucked that up by fighting with his friend.

She grabbed her phone and started googling drywallers. She stared at the list of companies, debating whether to start calling now or wait until Everett left. The polite thing to do would be to wait until he left, but Everett believing she was polite was a ship that had already sailed.

She clicked on the Yelp reviews for the first company. She immediately rejected them when over a dozen one-star reviews complained about the lack of communication and the time it took to finish a job.

She moved on to the next one, trying not to curse with frustration when they had nearly twenty-five one-star reviews. Christ, she was in so much trouble.

"Ms. Lewis?" Everett's annoyingly sexy voice was back.

She pasted on a smile and set her phone on the table. "Hi. That didn't take long."

"It's not good news, I'm afraid," he said. "Both walls are beyond being patched, and I don't believe the leak has been properly fixed. The drywall will need to be completely removed so the source of the water damage can be identified. Once a plumber has fixed that, new drywall can be installed."

"Okay," she said. She was disappointed but not surprised. "Thank you, Mr. Caine."

"You're welcome," he said. "I can start removing the drywall Monday morning if that suits your schedule."

She stared at him, shock rendering her voiceless.

"I realize you're trying to do as many renovations yourself as possible, but removing the drywall is best left to a professional. It can expose you to mold and a significant amount of drywall dust," Everett said.

"Right, no, I…that isn't… I mean…" Shit, she sounded like every brain cell had disintegrated.

Everett gave her a look. "What?"

"I assumed you wouldn't take the job," she said. "Because of what happened earlier at Home Depot."

"When you insulted me, you mean," he said.

She immediately bristled despite her best intentions. "No, when you didn't mind your own business."

His polite smile turned chilly. "The threaded wall anchors were incorrect for the job. I didn't think mentioning that would be an issue."

"Because we women are so dumb at this stuff, right?" she said. "Even when she works at Home Depot."

"It isn't about that," he said. "People make mistakes. She made a mistake. I pointed it out because I was trying to help."

"Except you were wrong," she said before pointing to the shelf of cookbooks. "The shelf is up, and the anchors are holding nicely despite the weight of the cookbooks, so the next time you -"

The splintering crash of the shelf falling off the wall was the absolute cherry on the shit sundae that was her fucking day.

She closed her eyes. Took a deep breath. Released it.

"So," Everett's sexy voice said, "does Monday morning work for you?"

"Hey, babe. Sorry, I'm late." Sierra kissed Indie's cheek. "I brought homemade brownies as an apology."

"You have nothing to apologize for," Indie said. "You're barely late."

"Where is everyone?" Sierra asked.

"In the backyard. Val decided to grill the steaks since it's so nice out. We set up the patio furniture so we could also eat out there. When did you have time to make brownies?"

"Yeah, I didn't," Sierra said. "They're store-bought, but the plate is from my house, so that makes them homemade, right?"

"Totally." Julia, their favourite server from their favourite restaurant and Val's daughter, joined them, throwing her arm around Indie. "Hey, Sierra."

"Hi, Julia. Wait, should I be calling you Raven now?" Sierra said.

Julia laughed. "You can call me Julia. I mean, technically, it's my name, just my middle name."

"Right, but Val always calls you Raven," Sierra said.

"He does, but," Julia gave Indie a cute smile, "Mom calls me Julia or Raven, and I answer to either. Right, Mom?"

"It's true," Indie said.

"How's school going?" Sierra asked.

"Almost finished for the summer, thank God," Julia said. "I'm so ready for a break. Did Mom tell you I'm going to Europe for two months?"

"She did," Sierra said.

"Dad is acting cool about it, but I know he's freaking out inside. But I'm twenty-one now, and he can't really stop me," Julia said. "Besides, I'm being, like, so safe about it. An entire group of people is going, and we have a plan in place for every possible disaster scenario. Including a zombie apocalypse."

"Always good to be prepared," Sierra said.

"Here, I'll take the brownies outside." Julia took the plate of brownies and headed toward the kitchen.

"She's calling you mom now?" Sierra said.

Indie nodded. "She had an earnest discussion with Val and me when I moved in last month about how she thought it would be appropriate to call me mom, but only if I was comfortable with it."

"That's adorable," Sierra said.

"It is," Indie said. "She's amazing, and honestly, since her dad and I started dating, I've only grown to love her more than I already did before I knew she was Val's daughter."

"I'm never gonna get over the whole her name is Julia, no it isn't, it's Raven, thing," Sierra said. "If Michaela changed her name, I'd be devastated."

Indie laughed. "Raven didn't change her name. She just started going by her middle name in university."

"Right, I remember," Sierra said. "Childhood trauma of being called crow."

"Listen," Indie's voice turned conspiratorial, "Val's best friend Mac is here, and I think the two of you would get along really well. If you know what I mean."

"You want me to bang Val's best friend?" Sierra asked.

Indie's cheeks turned pink like Sierra knew they would. "No, but you're single, and he's single, so maybe there would be a spark. How do you feel about macrame?"

"Why?" Sierra said.

Hazel's soft laugh came from behind Indie. "Mac is an expert at macrame. Hi, honey."

She hugged Sierra before handing her a glass of wine.

"Thank you." Sierra chugged all of it and wiped her mouth with the back of her hand.

"What?" she asked when Indie and Hazel looked at each other.

"What's wrong?" Indie asked.

"There's nothing wrong," Sierra said.

"You just chugged an entire glass of wine," Hazel said. "Something's wrong."

Sierra sighed. "Other than being horribly humiliated, it's been a fine fucking day."

"Uh oh." Indie took her arm and tugged her toward the kitchen. "C'mon, tell us what happened while I make the salad."

Fifteen minutes later, Sierra was on her second glass of wine, and both Indie and Hazel were giving her identical looks of sympathy mixed with just a touch of amusement.

"Man, I can't believe the shelf fell at that exact moment," Indie said. "That's some perfectly terrible timing, right there."

"Tell me about it," Sierra sighed.

A grey tabby cat walked into the kitchen, and Sierra nudged him gently with her foot. "Hello, Twig."

The cat growled and swatted her leg through her jeans. Sierra pulled her leg back before Twig could really dig his claws in. "I see moving into Val's place hasn't mellowed out Twig."

"Nope," Indie said with a laugh. "Although he is in love with the bunnies. It's ridiculously adorable to see him with Jack and Lulu. He grooms them, and they groom him back. Val hovered over them for the first week every time we brought all three into the living room. He was certain Twig would have a bunny snack, but Twig is weirdly gentle with them."

"So, Everett is starting to remove the drywall on Monday?" Hazel asked.

Sierra nodded. "Yes, which means I need to find a reliable plumber quickly to fix the possible water damage before Everett starts his next job. As it is, he'll only have time this go around to drywall the bathroom. I'll have to book him in the fall for the basement."

"It's a good thing, I guess, that he's so booked up. It means he's the best, right?" Indie said.

"Yes. I'm grateful that Hendrix recommended him, even if Everett is super smug and annoying," Sierra said.

Hazel laughed. "He came across as so quiet when I met him. I didn't get a smug asshole vibe at all."

"I might have, maybe, just a titch, taken out my irritation with Gary on Everett at Home Depot," Sierra said. "But I stand by him being annoying. The look on his face when that shelf fell… it was killing him not to say anything."

"But he didn't," Hazel said.

"True," Sierra said. "He gets half a point for that."

Hazel and Indie laughed as Sierra sighed. "Do you know what the worst part is? Despite how irritating I find him, I still want to fuck him. He's just so good looking, and that voice… and that ass… and those hands. His hands are… like, I can picture them turning my ass red, and it's delicious."

"Oh my God," Indie said, her face bright red. "You know the others are just past that door, right?" She pointed to the sliding doors that led out to the backyard.

Sierra shrugged. "No shame in liking what you like in the bedroom, babe."

"God, I wish I could be as open and casual about the sex stuff as you are," Indie said. "I mean, I'm way better than I used to be, thanks to Val, but I'm not as brave as you are, Sierra."

"It's less brave and more, I'm too old to give a shit anymore," Sierra said. "But take it from your elder, there's a lot of freedom in not giving a shit."

"Again, you're forty-six and only a year older than us," Hazel said. "Stop acting like you're ancient."

Sierra laughed. "Fine."

"And not to be a downer, but sleeping with Everett is probably a bad idea. What if he's terrible at it, and you don't want to sleep with him again? That'll be all kinds of awkward when you need him to drywall your basement," Hazel said.

"Uh, his wife is a bigger issue for not fucking him," Sierra said. "I'm a lot of things, but I'm not a homewrecker."

Hazel stared at her. "Everett isn't married. Is he?"

"He wears a wedding ring," Sierra said.

"I'm sure Hendrix said he was divorced," Hazel said.

The patio door slid open, and Hendrix stepped inside. "Ladies, mind if I interrupt to get another round of beers?"

"Not at all," Indie said. "They're on the bottom shelf of the fridge."

Hendrix stopped next to Hazel and gave her ass a quick squeeze before dropping a kiss on her mouth. "Hey, beautiful."

"Hi, honey. Hey, is Everett married?"

"Nope, he's divorced and has been for a while." Hendrix opened the fridge and bent over to grab the beers.

Sierra studied his ass as Indie nudged her and gave her a look. Sierra grinned and gave Hazel two thumbs up and an eyebrow wiggle. Hazel laughed, and Hendrix, his voice muffled by the fridge, said, "You guys are staring at my ass, right?"

"We are, and it's magnificent," Sierra said.

Hendrix straightened and grinned at her. "Thanks. I told

Preston that these jeans made my ass look good, and he said I had a dad butt, and it was impossible to make it look good."

Sierra laughed. "Michaela told me once that every pair of jeans I owned were mom jeans solely because they covered my ass crack."

"Kids, man," Hendrix said. He smiled at Hazel. "Speaking of Preston, he just texted. He and Spencer are coming over tomorrow afternoon for cribbage and nachos."

"Okay. You're positive that Everett didn't get remarried?" Hazel said.

"Yes," Hendrix said. "Why?"

"Just curious," Hazel said.

Hendrix left with the beers, and Hazel said, "See, I told you he wasn't married."

"He was wearing a wedding ring," Sierra said, "I'm sure of it."

The patio door opened, and Val stuck his head in. "The steaks are almost ready, doc."

Indie smiled at him. "Thanks, honey. I'm just finishing up the salad. We'll be right out."

He closed the door, and Indie picked up the salad bowl. "Sierra, would you be cool with me sitting you next to Mac during dinner?"

Sierra laughed. "You're determined to make this Mac thing happen, aren't you?"

Indie shrugged. "Mac's a great guy, and I think you two would get along well. And on a personal note, it would be awesome for me if my best friend was dating Val's best friend."

"Well, in that case, sit me next to Mac, and I'll get my flirt on," Sierra said with a grin.

CHAPTER 4

E verett stuck his head into Sierra's kitchen. Her back was turned to him, and her phone was to her ear as she stared out the window over the sink.

He watched her fingers turn white as she squeezed the edge of the farmhouse sink. "Are you absolutely sure you have nothing available for tomorrow? No, I realize it's last minute, but I didn't -"

Her fingers tap-tap-tapped a rapid beat on the counter as she listened. She reached behind her and scratched her upper thigh just below the curve of her ass cheek, and Everett studied her ass clad in tight yoga pants. Fuck, she had a great ass.

"No, I get that, but the wall has been taken down, and my drywall guy says it looks like a pretty standard pipe leak and shouldn't take more than a few hours to replace the pipe," she said.

More silence and Everett couldn't help but grin when Sierra, her voice so icy it would have made the Arctic cold, said, "No, I don't believe he does plumbing on the side, but I trust his judgment, and he's a fuck of a lot more helpful than you are, asshole."

She stabbed the end button on her phone and dropped it on the counter before saying in a low voice, "Motherfucking cocksucker. I hope you have to deal with shit-clogged toilets all fucking week."

His grin widened. He didn't know how it was possible, but Sierra swearing like a sailor turned him on even more.

He leaned against the doorway as Sierra ran her hands through her dark hair before downing the glass of lemonade sitting next to her phone. He'd just finished his cleanup from tearing down the bathroom walls and needed to leave before he was late for his dinner with Hendrix.

Of course, as much as he liked Hendrix, staring at Sierra's perfect ass was a fuck of a lot more fun.

Stop it, you creeper. One, she's your customer. Two, she kind of hates you, and three, even if the first two weren't true, and she wanted to fuck you, the first time you tried to take control in the bedroom, she'd tell you to go fuck yourself and boot your ass out of her bed. She's a control freak through and through.

She grabbed her phone with another muttered curse and typed rapidly. He studied the cookbooks still piled on the table and the wooden shelf leaning against the wall.

The shelf had ripped two large holes in the wall when it fell, and, he grinned a little, she'd need to patch the drywall and repaint before she could rehang the shelf.

Would she ask him to do it? He barely knew Sierra but didn't even have to consider the answer. Sierra would cut off a finger before she'd ask him to patch the wall.

She turned and twitched when she saw him in the doorway. She set her phone on the counter and fixed a polite smile on her face. "All finished, Mr. Caine?"

"Like I said before, it's Everett, and yes, I'm finished with the cleanup," he said.

"Right, thank you so much. If you want to give me your invoice, I'll get my credit card," she said.

"I don't normally invoice until the job is finished," he said. "I'll have the new drywall installed and mudded on Wednesday and do the sanding on Friday. I can give you the invoice when I'm finished on Friday."

A pinched look came over her face, and he had the inappropriate urge to cross the kitchen and try to smooth away the little lines from between her eyebrows. Her usual fiery personality had dissolved in the blink of an eye, leaving behind a pretty but wilting flower.

She rubbed at the back of her neck. "Right, about that. I couldn't find a plumber to fix the leaking pipe tomorrow, so I'm afraid I won't be able to have you install new drywall this week. I realize you'll have a cancellation fee, and I'm happy to pay it. Just add it to the invoice today."

"If I don't do it this week, I won't have availability to install the drywall until the fall," he said.

"I'm aware," she snapped before making a face. "I apologize. I'm being a dick."

"I could install the drywall on Thursday and sand on Saturday," he said. "That'll give you an extra day to find a plumber."

"You don't work weekends," she said, those little lines deepening between her eyebrows. "Hendrix was clear about that when he recommended you."

"I can make an exception," he said.

"Why?" she said.

"Do I need a reason?" he asked.

"It's just a question," she said.

He refrained from rolling his eyes. Christ, this woman.

One minute he wanted to fuck her against the wall, and the next, he wanted to put her over his knee and spank the attitude right out of her.

Why not both?

"Maybe I'm offering because I'm not the asshole you seem determined to think I am," he said. "But I'm happy to enjoy my Saturday off if my offer offended you."

She sighed. "Fuck, I'm being such a dick again. I apologize. It's been a stressful day, and I shouldn't take it out on you. I appreciate your offer and will happily accept it."

"Text me tomorrow night and let me know if you've found a plumber for Wednesday," he said.

"Okay," she said. "Are you sure you're good with giving up your Saturday?"

"Yes," he said.

"Maybe you should check with your wife first," she said, her gaze dropping to his bare left hand.

"I'm not married," he said.

"Then why were you wearing a wedding ring on Friday?" she asked and then had the good grace to look embarrassed. "Sorry, that's none of my business."

"Handsy client," he said.

She blinked at him. "I'm sorry?"

"My client last week was a seventy-two-year-old divorcee who was handsy as fuck with me the first day I worked at her house."

At last, those small lines between her eyebrows disappeared. "You're kidding me?"

"I'm not," he said. "I returned the second day wearing my fake wedding ring and praising my non-existent wife's cooking from the night before and had a lot less ass-grabbing to contend with."

Sierra grinned before giving him a look. "Wait, a lot less... it didn't stop altogether?"

"Not completely. She was," he paused and decided to say it, "very horny."

Sierra's genuine laughter warmed him to his fucking toes. It also threatened to make him hard as a fucking rock.

"Oh my God," she said, "I'm sorry, I shouldn't laugh. Sexual harassment isn't funny, but I keep picturing you trying to drywall and a little old lady creeping up behind you to grab your ass."

"That's exactly what it looked like. The first time she did it, I screamed like a virgin in a horror movie and spilled drywall mud everywhere," he said.

Sierra laughed so hard she had to grab onto the counter for support.

"She gave me a four-star review on Yelp," Everett said. "Pretty sure if I'd let her grab my ass whenever she wanted, it would have been five. But I'm not that much of a Yelp star whore."

Sierra laughed again, her body shaking with the exertion before she got control of herself. "I'm glad my job is not dependent on Yelp reviews."

He really needed to leave. With traffic, he'd be lucky if he was only fifteen minutes late for dinner. Instead, he settled more firmly against the door jamb and said, "What do you do?"

"I'm a judge," she said.

Disappointment rocketed through him, but he shoved it deep before it could reach the surface for her to see. It wasn't a big deal, right? It's not like he had a chance with her anyway. Finding out she was way above his socioeconomic status shouldn't mean anything to him.

"What?" she said. "Why do you have that look on your face? Are you surprised I'm a judge?"

"Oh, I'm definitely *not* surprised by that," he said.

"What's that supposed to mean?"

"It means you're good at quickly judging people," he said teasingly.

The smile dropped off her face, and she gave him a cool nod. "Right. Thank you again for being so flexible with your schedule this week. I'll let you know by tomorrow evening if I find a plumber."

Shit. He hadn't meant to offend her. "Ms. Lewis, I didn't mean -"

"I don't want to be rude, but I have an engagement this evening that I need to get ready for," she said.

Feeling like the asshole he'd just said he wasn't, he nodded and pushed away from the door jamb. "Have a nice evening."

"You as well, Mr. Caine."

"You know nothing good ever comes from fucking a client." Hendrix took a swallow of beer, grinning at how Everett choked on his bite of burger.

"I'm not fucking a client," Everett said when he no longer felt like he needed the Heimlich maneuver.

"Not yet, but you want to fuck Sierra Lewis," Hendrix said.

"Uh, no, I don't." The back of Everett's neck heated up.

"We've been friends for fifteen years, Everett. I know you're 'I want to fuck that woman' look. You know she's a judge, right?"

"I do. Why?"

Hendrix shrugged. "I don't think she's your type, is all."

"I *know* she isn't," Everett said. "We butt heads every time we're in the same room."

"I meant more in the bedroom," Hendrix said. "I haven't known Sierra for that long, but she likes control."

"She does," Everett said. "That's obvious."

Hendrix twirled some pasta onto his fork before eating it. "Maybe she doesn't want control in the bedroom. That's a thing, right? One way in the bedroom, complete opposite out of it?"

Everett laughed. "It's been my experience that is *not* a thing. If a woman takes charge in her everyday life, she's like that in the bedroom, too."

"Probably for the best. Fucking a client is never a good idea."

"You already said that," Everett said, "and it's not like I'm a green kid on my first job, Hendrix. Christ, give me some credit."

"I know you're not, but I also know how hard it is to resist someone even when you can't be with them. No matter how hard I tried, I couldn't stay away from Hazel."

"Even if my attraction to Sierra were reciprocated, it wouldn't be more than one night. Women like her don't slum for long."

Hendrix frowned at him. "Sierra isn't like that. Don't let your past start fucking with your head again, Everett."

"I'm not," Everett said. "I'm being realistic. Sierra is a judge, and I guarantee her paycheque is twice the size of mine. I don't care about that, but she would."

"You're making a hell of a lot of assumptions, my friend," Hendrix said.

"They aren't assumptions," Everett said, "and you know it. Rich, powerful women like Sierra Lewis are happy to bed us blue-collar boys, but that's as far as it goes. They wouldn't be caught dead with us in public."

"Sierra isn't Wendy," Hendrix said. "They're nothing alike, in fact."

"You just said you didn't know Sierra that well," Everett said.

"No, but I know Hazel, and she wouldn't be friends with Sierra if Sierra were a snob about social status and wealth."

"It doesn't matter because she's a client, and I don't sleep with clients," Everett said.

A young woman with long dark hair in a ponytail and wearing a Dawson's name tag, joined them at their table. "Hendrix! Hey!"

"Hi, Julia. How are you?" Hendrix asked.

"I'm good. You should have texted Mom that you were eating here tonight. I would have had the hostess put you in my section," she said.

"I will next time," Hendrix said. "This is my friend, Everett. Everett, this is Julia."

"Hi, Julia. Nice to meet you," Everett said.

"You too," Julia said cheerfully. "Hendrix, are you still joining my dad and Uncle Mac at poker night this Friday?"

"I am," he said. "Where I fully expect to lose all of my money."

She laughed. "Don't let Dad and Uncle Mac get into your head. They're not as good at poker as they think they are. Their friend Trevor usually cleans house... he's the one you have to watch out for."

"Good to know," Hendrix said.

"Anyway, I should get back to work. It was, like, really great to see you. Give Hazel my love." She gave his shoulder a friendly squeeze before leaving.

"She seems like a sweet kid," Everett said.

"She is," Hendrix said. "She's Hazel's best friend's boyfriend's daughter."

"Right," Everett said.

Hendrix laughed. "It's not as confusing as it sounds."

"I'll take your word for it." He studied his friend. "Hey, I'm really happy for you and Preston. You know that, right? Hazel seems like a great woman, and it's good that your social life is picking up. You were spending too much time alone."

"Thanks, man. Hazel has changed my and Preston's life for the better. It can be a little awkward around new people when they find out that our kids are engaged to each other as well, but the four of us decided we didn't care what others think."

"You shouldn't," Everett said firmly. "You and Preston deserve happiness."

Hendrix studied him. "So do you, Everett."

"I'm happy."

"Are you? You spend more time alone than I did before I met Hazel."

"Work keeps me busy," Everett said.

"It can't just be all work all the time," Hendrix said. "You aren't having luck with the dating app?"

Everett snorted. "I deleted it six months ago when I realized that most of the women on the over fifty dating app were women in their twenties looking for a 'daddy'. I like control in the bedroom but don't have a daddy kink. The only person I want calling me daddy is my kid."

"How's Taylor doing?" Hendrix asked. "Is she still in Tokyo?"

"Yes. She decided to do another year of teaching English as a second language. She loves her students and the city and says her itch to travel hasn't been completely scratched yet."

Hendrix laughed. "Well, that's good for her but not so great for you."

"I miss her like crazy," Everett admitted. "When she was home at Christmas, it was tough not trying to talk her out of teaching for another year. But she's happy, and I won't be that selfish person who makes her feel guilty for living her dream."

"Like Wendy?" Hendrix said.

Everett sighed. "Yeah. Wendy is laying the guilt on thick about Taylor staying another year in Tokyo, but Taylor's standing strong. I'm proud of her. Her relationship with her mom hasn't always been the healthiest, and Taylor's come a long way since she moved to Japan."

Hendrix leaned back in the booth, a small smile on his face. "I seriously never thought I could be as proud of someone as I am of Preston. Being a dad changed my life for the better."

"Mine too," Everett said. "Even with how badly it went between Wendy and me, I can't regret it. Not when it gave me Taylor."

"I get it," Hendrix said. "And as happy as I am that Taylor is finding her own path, it means you're alone more than you should be."

"I'm fine," Everett said.

"Get back on the dating app," Hendrix said. "You're too goddamn young to give up on finding your person."

"Christ, being with Hazel has turned you into an adorable love-sick fool," Everett said.

Hendrix laughed. "I just want my friends to be as happy as I am."

"I'm happy," Everett said.

Hendrix gave him a look that practically screamed how

skeptical he was but dropped the subject. He ate another few bites of pasta as Everett pushed his fries around his plate.

Was he lonely? Sure, maybe a little, but he was happy. Or at least content. He was glad Hendrix had found a second chance at love, but he was only forty-eight. At fifty-six, Everett's chance of finding someone narrowed with every year.

He'd had his chance with Wendy, and it hadn't worked out. Finding someone his age now who shared his interests both inside the bedroom and out was a long shot.

An image of Sierra flashed in his head, and he grimaced inwardly. He was barking up the wrong fucking tree, even fantasizing about his sexy but frustrating new client.

CHAPTER 5

"Your honour, I must strenuously object to your decision to send my client back to -"

Sierra held up her hand. "Enough, counsel. You've made your position clear many times. I'm not changing my mind."

The defense counsel, a pale and bloated man with thinning hair, a loud voice, and a nasty habit of badgering witnesses to tears, stood and buttoned his suit jacket with hard, jabbing motions. In a voice dripping with barely controlled fury, he said, "I'll be filing my appeal this afternoon."

"You do that," she said dismissively, turning to stare at her computer screen.

She waited until he left her chambers, not quite daring to slam the door but closing it hard enough to make his point, before she sat back in her chair and rubbed at her forehead.

It'd been a busy morning, and she seriously considered grabbing her book and escaping to the nearby park to decompress over her lunch hour. Instead, she dug her phone out of her purse. She needed to spend her lunch hour calling plumbers. Not that she thought she'd have any luck finding one for Wednesday, but she had to try. Especially since Everett had been nice enough to postpone his schedule to accommodate her.

It was so nice of him. You should say thanks by fucking him.

She rolled her eyes. She honestly regretted confirming that Everett wasn't married. Her inner voice hadn't shut the fuck up about banging him since.

You weren't complaining last night when we masturbated our way to multiple orgasms with fantasies starring Everett and those big hands of his.

Okay, maybe she had allowed herself a few harmless fantasies about fucking the drywaller, but that's all they were… fantasies. He found her annoying and judgmental as hell, and she found him irritating, too.

Irritating and sexy.

"Shut up," she muttered to herself.

Her cell rang, and "Fernandez Plumbing" appeared on the screen. Frowning, she hit the answer button. "Sierra Lewis speaking."

"Hello, this is Erica from Fernandez Plumbing. I'm calling to confirm your three-thirty appointment tomorrow."

"I'm sorry?" Sierra said.

"Your appointment," Erica said patiently. "Isabelle will be there at three thirty."

"I don't… I didn't book an appointment," Sierra said. "Did I?"

There was a pause, and then Erica said, "I have you on our schedule for tomorrow. Hold, please."

There was a click, and crappy hold music drifted into her ear. Sierra pulled her phone away and stared at the screen. "What is happening?"

The music cut out, and she pressed the phone to her ear. A

different woman, who had a soft Spanish accent, said, "Ms. Lewis?"

"Yes?"

"I'm Isabelle Fernandez."

"Uh, hello. I think there must be some mistake. I didn't schedule an appointment with your company. I mean, I need a plumber for tomorrow, desperately, in fact, but I didn't book an appointment."

Isabelle laughed. "Typical of Everett not to tell you."

"Everett... wait, do you mean my drywaller Everett Caine?" Sierra said.

"That's the one," Isabelle said with another laugh. "He called me this morning, summarized what was going on, and asked me to squeeze you in today or tomorrow. He obviously didn't tell you."

"He didn't," Sierra said.

"Like I said, typical Everett," Isabelle said with amusement. "Anyway, three thirty tomorrow is the only time I can fix the pipe, so I hope that works for you."

"I can absolutely make it work," Sierra said. "Thank you so much. I appreciate it."

"De nada," Isabelle said. "Everett's helped me out more than once. I'm happy to return the favour. See you tomorrow."

She ended the call, and Sierra studied her phone before scrolling her text messages to Everett's name. She hesitated briefly before sending him a text.

SIERRA

> Thank you for reaching out to Isabelle. She's coming by tomorrow at three-thirty to fix the pipe.

She set her phone on her desk, snatching it up again when

she saw the three dots appear. Her heart beating much too hard, she chewed at her bottom lip, reading Everett's message when it appeared.

EVERETT

You're welcome. Glad she could fit you in.

Feeling weirdly disappointed by the briefness of the message, Sierra stuck her phone in her purse, grabbed her book from her desk drawer, and left her chambers.

———

"Oh my God, Sierra, be so happy you said no to the farmer's market." Indie sounded both amused and exasperated. "It's way too hot and insane with people."

Sierra shifted her phone to her other ear as she squeezed the last lemon into the glass jug in front of her. "It's the first Saturday of the season. Of course it's insane."

"There's a booth that sells the cutest ceramic chickens. Julia and I are trying to convince Val he needs one for his kitchen. Well, our kitchen now, I guess," Indie said.

Sierra could hear the faint sound of Julia's voice. "Ooh, good point. You gotta get the ceramic chicken for her, Dad. It's her kitchen, too, you know."

Indie laughed. "I wish you could see Val's face right now, Sierra."

"I take it he isn't into ceramic chickens?" Sierra added water to the jug, some lemon slices, and a cup of sugar before stirring it with a long wooden spoon.

"Apparently not," Indie said. "How's the drywalling going?"

"Good, I think," Sierra said. "He installed the new sheets

and mudded on Thursday, so it's just the sanding today. He's been here for a few hours, and I assume it's going well."

"Good. You still want to bang him?"

"Indiana!" Sierra said, grinning when Indie burst into giggles.

"What?" Indie said between giggles. "It's just a question."

"Said in front of Val and his kid," Sierra said.

"Nah, they're looking at ceramic chickens," Indie said. "So, do you still want to have sex with him or what?"

"Sadly, yes," Sierra said before changing the subject. "Do you know if Hazel and Hendrix made it to the cabin last night?"

"They did. Hazel sent me a text. It's just as warm there as it is here. No issues with the drive up the mountain."

"Good. What are you doing tonight? Do you want to have a girl's night?"

"Shoot, Val, and I are taking a bike ride to Bathwood as soon as we're done here and will probably spend the night," Indie said. "But we could do that next weekend. Give me five minutes to talk to Val and -"

"No, don't be silly," Sierra said. "Go have fun with your bad biker bunny guy."

"Are you sure?" Indie said. "I'm worried I haven't been a very good friend since Val and I started dating."

"I'm the one being a bad friend. I'm too busy with renovations and have cancelled plans on you and Hazel a few times," Sierra said.

"We understand, honey," Indie said. "So, don't worry about it one bit. Hey, did you hear from Mac? I gave him your cell number."

Sierra groaned. "Indie, you didn't."

"I did. Why? I thought you two were getting along great at the barbeque."

"He seems like a great guy, and I wouldn't say no to a date, but he didn't ask for my number, so he obviously wasn't interested."

"Mac's shy," Indie said.

Sierra laughed. "No, he isn't, Indiana."

She sighed. "Okay, fine, he isn't. Sorry, honey, I was hoping there would be a spark."

"Eh, you win some, you lose some, right? If Mac's not interested, he's not interested. Anyway, you should get your ceramic chicken before they sell out. Love you, babe."

"Love you too, Sierra," Indie said, ending the call.

Sierra stirred the lemonade and gave it a quick taste before adding a few more lemon slices to the jug and stirring again. She poured a glass of lemonade and, her heart thumping, left the kitchen and headed up the stairs.

She was bringing Everett lemonade because it was an unseasonably warm day, drywalling was hot and dusty work, and she was a nice person.

It wasn't because she wanted to check out his ass or wanted an excuse to hear his sexy as fuck voice. Nope, that wasn't it. Because as good looking as he was, he was also kind of annoying, and he definitely found her irritating, so it's not like he'd be so grateful for the lemonade that he'd offer to fuck her, right?

She'd hired Everett to drywall, not take her against the wall.

Too bad her stupid lady bits hadn't gotten the message yet.

She walked down the hall and toward her bedroom. Everett, his skin and shirt covered in drywall dust and a dust mask pulled up to sit on top of his head, stood near the soaker tub still taking up space in her bedroom. He was studying his phone, and she cleared her throat. "Mr. Caine, I brought you some – oh fuck!"

The toolbox she'd just tripped over tipped onto its side, spilling various tools and screws and bolts onto the tile floor. She might have been okay and saved herself and the glass of lemonade if she hadn't stepped directly on the screwdriver. She fell forward, the lemonade shooting out of the glass to spray all over Everett as Sierra slammed into him with the grace of a newborn zebra.

He caught her with a grunt, and she had just enough time to register how fucking good he smelled before they both fell into her new soaker tub, and she landed on him in a tangle of limbs and curses, whacking her head on the side of the tub.

Sprawled on top of Everett, her ears ringing and pain radiating out of her skull, she squinted at him when he said, "Jesus, are you okay?"

"I made you lemonade," she said. She stared at his shirt. The lemonade soaked into it was now tinged a weird pink colour. "Not strawberry lemonade, though."

She touched the wet material as Everett skimmed his fingers over her head.

"Ouch." Even that gentle touch hurt like a son of a bitch. She stared at Everett. "Why do you look like you're freaking out?"

Oh shit… those were blood drops on his shirt.

With visions of Everett needing to go to the hospital, but not before he promised to sue the shit out of her racing through her head, she touched his chest. "You're bleeding. Tell me where you're hurt. Can you sit up? Here, I'll help you sit up."

"Sierra, stop." Everett's arm anchored around her waist, preventing her from moving. "I'm not bleeding. You are."

CHAPTER 6

"Almost finished, Ms. Lewis." The doctor, who looked about fourteen with a wispy mustache and a few patches of hair on his jaw masquerading as a beard, adjusted the light before bending over Sierra again.

Everett squeezed Sierra's hand. He'd sat beside the hospital bed and taken Sierra's hand as soon as Sierra had gasped with pain from the needle used to numb the area.

He couldn't see Sierra's face, thanks to the surgical cloth that covered her head and face, but she squeezed his hand in return, her short and sensible nails digging into the top of his hand.

The doctor made his final suture before cutting the excess and cleaning the area. He removed the cloth and smiled at Sierra. "Eight stitches, not bad."

"Thanks," Sierra said with a grimace. She used her free hand to touch her blood-caked hair. "Can I wash my hair when I get home?"

He nodded. "Sure, just be gentle with the washing and rinse it well."

He took off his gloves and tossed them into the garbage

can before turning to Everett. "You'll need to watch your wife tonight for signs of a concussion."

"He's my drywaller, not my husband," Sierra said.

The doctor's gaze dropped to their linked hands. "Oh, okay."

Sierra let go of Everett's hand, and he had the sudden and inappropriate urge to punch the Doogie Howser wannabe.

"So, you'll need someone to stay with you for the next twenty-four hours to watch for concussion symptoms," the doctor said.

"I feel fine," Sierra said. "No headache or nausea."

"That's good," he said, "but symptoms can develop hours after hitting your head. So, it's best to have someone stay with you to monitor you."

"Should she be woken up every hour tonight?" Everett asked.

The doctor shook his head. "Not necessary. It's a myth about waking up someone with a concussion every hour. That being said, checking on her once or twice at night to ensure she isn't having symptoms is recommended."

He pushed back his rolling stool and stood. "If you do develop a headache, nausea, blurred vision, or confusion, come back to urgent care or go to emergency if it's after hours. Okay?"

"All right," Sierra said. "Thank you."

"You're welcome." The doctor left the room, and Sierra sat up with a grimace. She touched her hair again and made a face. "Gross."

"Come on, let's get you home," Everett said.

He stood, acutely aware of Sierra's soft hand when she grabbed his wrist. "Thank you for driving me to urgent care and staying, Mr. Caine."

He arched an eyebrow at her. "I have your blood all over my shirt. I think we can be on a first name basis, don't you?"

She nodded, her face too pale for his liking. "Yes. Thank you, Everett."

"You're welcome, Sierra."

"Thank you for the ride home." Sierra eased her body into the kitchen chair. She still looked pale and tired, and Everett squatted in front of her.

"Sierra, do you feel nauseous?"

"No, and no headache either. I'm good, really."

He doubted that, but he didn't press.

"I'm sorry I interrupted your sanding." Sierra glanced at the microwave clock. They'd had a long wait at the urgent care, and it was almost seven.

"I was just finishing up when you came into the bedroom," he said. "Nothing left but clean up."

"Oh, okay, that's good." She rubbed the back of her neck. "I'm happy for you to come back to do clean up if you'd rather not do it tonight. Or, I can do the clean up for you tomorrow since it's my fault you've been here all day."

He shook his head. "I'll clean up while I wait for your person to show up."

"Sorry?" she said.

"The person you're calling to stay the night with you," he said. "I'm not leaving until they get here."

"Oh, uh," her gaze cut to the left, "that's okay. They live close, so it won't take them long to get here. Head on home."

"I'll wait," he said.

"I'm sure you're starving and want to," her gaze dropped

to his chest, "get out of that sticky, blood-stained shirt and shower. I'll be fine until my friend gets here."

"Sierra," he said.

She studied something over his shoulder. "What?"

"Call your friend right now while I'm here."

She glared at him. "I'm not a child, Everett. You can't tell me what to do."

"Sierra," he said.

"Fine. I don't have anyone to stay with me, okay? Indie is out of town, and so is Hazel. My parents live out of state, and my kid is away at university. That leaves no one but my ex-husband, and I'd rather die of a concussion before I call him."

He straightened and took her hands, helping her to stand. "Go have a hot shower while I order us some food. Do you like Greek?"

"I... what?"

"I'm staying the night," he said.

She stared wide-eyed at him. "You're not staying the night."

"Yeah, I am," he said.

"You can't just - just stay the night. I don't even know you," she said.

He grinned. "I'm Everett. I'm fifty-six years old, my hobbies include pottery and skiing, and I'm a Scorpio."

"Of course you're a Scorpio," she said.

He laughed. "You're a Capricorn, aren't you?"

She blinked at him. "How did you know that?"

"Capricorns are driven by a desire to achieve their goals," he said. "You seem very... goal-oriented."

"Do you really do pottery?" she asked.

"I do," he said. "If I had a huge backyard like you do here, I'd build a kiln for myself."

"Okay, that's kind of cool," she said begrudgingly.

"Don't hurt yourself with the compliments," he teased before pointing to the doorway. "Go have your shower while I order dinner."

"Everett, I…"

He shook his head. "I'm not budging on this, Sierra. You can't be alone tonight."

"At least let me buy dinner," she said.

He shook his head. "It's my treat. Go shower, Sierra. Your head is very bloody and gross to look at."

She smiled. It was faint, and he didn't love how exhausted she looked, but it was better than nothing. "Okay."

———

SIERRA COULD HEAR EVERETT'S FOOTSTEPS ON THE STAIRS, and she gripped the sink and stared out the window.

Okay, girl, prepare yourself. He'll be half-naked, and you absolutely cannot stare at his chest like a pervert.

She sucked in a deep breath. After her shower, Everett had gone upstairs to take one, and it's not like he would put his covered in blood, lemonade, and drywall dust shirt back on, right? And none of her shirts would come even close to fitting him.

Which meant he'd be shirtless.

While they ate dinner.

Which was perfectly fine. She could handle a little naked-ness at dinner.

You're assuming he has a great chest. Maybe he doesn't.

She wasn't holding her breath on that one. Everett had a habit of wearing his t-shirts tight, so she had a pretty good idea of his chest definition.

She pulled some plates from the cupboard and set them on the counter. The food had arrived while Everett was showering. She hadn't felt hungry before, but the smell of the moussaka made her stomach growl.

"The food smells delicious." Everett's sexy voice filled the kitchen.

She straightened her shoulders, put a smile on her face and turned around. "It does. Thank you again for ordering..."

"What's wrong?" Everett joined her at the counter.

"You're wearing a shirt," she said.

He glanced down at himself before giving her an amused look. "My mother would roll over in her grave if I was shirtless at the kitchen table."

"Right, no... I just thought because your other shirt was ruined, you would have to be... I mean, because you couldn't fit in my shirts..." Christ, she sounded like a blithering fool.

"I carry an extra set of clothes in my truck in case of drywall emergencies," he said with a grin.

"Yes, of course, that makes sense." She was staring at his fabric-covered chest and pushed her gaze to his face instead. "Well, that's good that you have extra clothes. In your truck. For emergencies."

"You sound disappointed," he said teasingly.

Her face flushed red. "I'm not."

"I can take this off if that's what you want," he grabbed the hem of his shirt, "and risk the wrath of my mama's ghost."

"I don't," she said. "You're not my type at all."

"Owch," he said with another grin.

"Fuck, I'm being rude. Sorry," she said.

"It's fine. Besides, I know you're fibbing about me not being your type."

She rolled her eyes. "Are you always this cocky around women?"

"I like to think of it as confident," he said. "How's your head feel?"

"Fine. It's still numb," she said.

"Any dizziness, headache, or nausea?"

"No," she said.

"Good." He stepped closer, and she leaned back against the counter.

"What are you doing?"

"Just checking to see how it looks." His rough fingers grasped her chin, and her lungs forgot how to do their job. She swallowed hard as he tugged her head down and studied the gash in her skull.

She stared at his chest, ignoring her urge to lean forward and rest her forehead against that muscular wall of delight. "How's it look?"

"Good," he said. "He did a nice job with the suturing, considering he was still in high school."

She laughed. "Right? I almost asked him where his mom was when he walked into the room."

He stepped back and grabbed the plates from the counter, setting them on the island. "One thing I wasn't prepared for in growing old was how damn young everyone else starts to look."

"Please. Fifty-six isn't old," she said.

He grinned at her as she handed him the utensils and the napkins. "That's easy to say when you're barely into your forties."

She opened the bag of food. "I'm not sure if this is you trying to flirt or if you really think I'm that young."

He pulled out the food from the bag. "There's no way you're older than forty-two."

"I'm forty-six," she said.

He paused with a container of moussaka in one big hand. "You're kidding me?"

"I'm not," she said.

His gaze dropped briefly down her body before he busied himself with opening the food containers. "You don't look forty-six."

"Thank you," she said. Even that brief look had made her feel too warm, and she refrained from fanning herself. Instead, she opened the fridge and said, "I have beer, lemonade, or water."

"Water for me," he said.

She poured them both glasses of water as he dished out the food onto the plates. There was an ease to their motions like this was something they'd done hundreds of times before and would do hundreds of times again.

He pulled out her stool for her, and she sat down, smiling tentatively at him when he sat next to her. "Thank you again, Everett. This is going above and beyond as a contractor."

He grinned at her. "You're welcome, Sierra. Now, eat up before the food gets cold."

CHAPTER 7

"This moussaka is delicious." Sierra ate another bite, her eyes nearly rolling up in her head at how good it was.

"It's my favourite Greek place in town," he said. "Not that we have a lot of places to choose from."

"Did you grow up here?" she asked.

"No, I grew up in Vermont," he said. "My parents moved here when I was sixteen. I didn't expect to stay, but I met my ex-wife, Wendy, during my senior year. She was born and raised in this town and had no intentions of leaving. How about you? Were you born here?"

"No, but my parents moved here when I was six, so it's been home for as long as I can remember. My ex, Gary, and I moved to Washington once I got my law degree because he was pursuing a political career. We moved back here when our daughter, Michaela, was ten."

"Did you want to move back?" he asked.

"Yes. I love small-town living and wanted Michaela to have the same experience. Also, I missed Hazel and Indie like crazy. We've been best friends since we were teens." She drank some water and wiped her mouth with her napkin. "Do you have kids?"

"I do. A daughter named Taylor. She's twenty-six and teaches English as a second language in Tokyo."

"Good for her. I assume she enjoys it?" Sierra asked.

"Very much. She was only supposed to teach for a year, but she told us at Christmas she was staying for another year. I was happy for her, but…"

"You miss her," Sierra said softly. Everett's face was a mixture of pride and sadness. She reached for his hand before thinking better of it and tucking her hands into a fist in her lap instead.

"A lot," he said. "Wendy was very motivated in her career, so after Taylor was born, I did the stay-at-home dad thing with her until she started school. We're probably a little closer than the average father and daughter."

"What does Wendy do?" Sierra asked.

"She's the chief of medicine at Bellevue Hospital," Everett said.

"Wow," Sierra said.

His face twisted, and the warmth in his eyes disappeared. "Yeah, I know. Shocking that she was with a guy like me."

She frowned. "I didn't say that."

"You didn't have to," he said.

"You're inferring a lot from a single 'wow'," she said.

He set down his fork and pinched the bridge of his nose. "You're right. I apologize."

There was a bit of awkward silence before he said, "You said Michaela was away at school?"

"Yes. Only a couple of hours away, and she comes home at least one weekend a month, so I know how lucky I am, but I still miss her like crazy. She's in the last year of her bachelor's degree in economics," Sierra said.

"Impressive."

"We're really proud of her. Her dad thought she was headed into a career in politics, but she's following in my footsteps and becoming a lawyer."

"Is your ex still in politics?" Everett asked.

"Yes. He's the mayor." She grinned at the look on Everett's face.

"Your ex-husband is Mayor Henson?" he asked.

"The one and only," she said.

"Is this where I tell you I voted for the other guy?" Everett asked.

"So did I," Sierra said.

Everett laughed, and Sierra's entire body tingled pleasantly. She could no longer remember why she'd found him so annoying.

Everett stood and started to clear the island. She slid off the stool and reached for her plate. He scooped it up before she could. "I'll clean up. Go relax on the couch."

"I feel fine," she said. "I can help."

"Trust me. You won't be fine when the numbing wears off," he said.

"But the numbing hasn't worn off," she said.

He rolled his eyes. "Sierra, stop arguing with me and relax on the couch."

"Fine, Mr. BossyPants," she said.

He laughed. "Takes one to know one."

She stuck her tongue out at him before leaving the kitchen. Her pulse raced, and she felt flushed and too warm again. God, how long had it been since she flirted like a teenager? Too long. Most of her relationships since her divorce had been little more than hookups arranged over dating apps with little to no flirting required.

The one guy she'd seriously dated since her divorce had

taken a job in another state about eight months into the relationship. Despite how much she liked him, she had just bought her new place and wasn't about to sell it and move, and she was too damn old for a long-distance relationship.

You shouldn't be flirting with Everett. He's your contractor.

Sure, but technically, the job was finished now.

He'll be back in the fall, remember?

She sighed and sank onto the couch, resting her head gingerly against the cushion. Her little rush from flirting had faded, and she was suddenly exhausted and depressed.

She made herself smile when Everett joined her, sinking onto the couch a respectable distance away. He studied her for only a few seconds before saying, "What's wrong?"

"Nothing," she said. "Long day."

He settled into the cushions, stretching his long legs out before him. "Not exactly how I expected it to go."

"You don't have to stay. I'll be fine," she said. "I'm confident if I had a concussion, symptoms would have shown up by now."

"I'm not leaving you alone, Sierra. You need someone to check on you through the night." A look crossed his face, and he shifted to face her. "Shit, I'm being an asshole. Are you nervous about me staying the night? Because I swear, this is me wanting to make sure you're okay. I know we don't know each other that well, but I promise I'm not going to do anything to -"

"Oh, oh God, no," she said quickly. "Everett, I'm not worried about that at all. I trust you. I just feel bad you're spending your Saturday night here when you could be out with friends."

The tension eased from his shoulders, and he smiled at

her. "I didn't have plans with friends tonight. I promise I want to be here, Sierra."

She chewed at her bottom lip. "Okay, well, thank you again. I really appreciate this."

"You're welcome." He glanced at the television. "So, I have a slight addiction to true crime documentaries, and there are a few on Netflix that I still haven't watched. How do you feel about them?"

She laughed. "I haven't watched that many, but I'm happy to give one a shot."

"Perfect," he said.

His grin of delight sent another wave of shivers over her and a real urge to find out what his lips tasted like.

Oh, girl, you are in so much trouble.

EVERETT PAUSED THE SHOW AND STUDIED SIERRA. AN HOUR ago, she had curled up in a small ball at her end of the couch to 'get more comfortable' and promptly fallen asleep. He'd covered her with the afghan draped across the back of the couch and finished watching the documentary.

He slid closer and rubbed her hip through the blanket. "Sierra, wake up."

She didn't move, and he shook her lightly. "Wake up, Sierra."

Still nothing, and panic bit at his insides. Shit. He pulled the afghan back and sat next to her on the couch. He shook her arm and squeezed it lightly. "Sierra, can you hear me?"

Her eyes rolled behind her lids, and he cupped her face. "Sierra, open your eyes."

Panic made his voice too loud, but it woke her up. She

squinted at him, and he slid his arm around her waist and urged her into a sitting position.

"What's wrong?" she mumbled.

"Do you feel okay?" He cupped her face and studied her eyes. They looked normal, and he stroked her silky cheek. "Do you feel dizzy?"

"No," she said, her gaze soft as she studied him. "No dizziness, no headache."

Relief swept through him, and he squeezed her hip. "Thank God. When you wouldn't wake up, I thought…"

She smiled sleepily at him. "I'm a deep sleeper."

"You are," he said, the relief evident in his voice.

He was still cupping her face, and he dropped his hand before he did something inappropriate like kiss her. She immediately leaned forward and pressed her mouth against his.

He shouldn't have returned her kiss, but he groaned at the touch of her soft lips and pulled her into his lap. She gripped the front of his t-shirt and kissed him again with soft and delicate brushes of her mouth against his.

He was already hard as a fucking stone, which was all kinds of embarrassing, but Sierra's warm body against his and how she traced his bottom lip with the tip of her tongue made him lose control.

He cupped the back of her neck and angled his mouth over hers, sliding his tongue into her mouth to taste and explore. She moaned softly, her hands pulling him closer as they kissed.

He slid his hand into her thick dark hair, registering his mistake a split second too late when his fingers pressed against the sutures in her scalp.

Sierra made a sharp cry of pain against his mouth, and he cursed inwardly before easing his hand out of her hair and leaning back.

"Fuck, I'm sorry."

"It's fine." She smiled at him, but he could see the pain lurking in it. "The numbing has worn off, so let's avoid touching my head."

She leaned forward to kiss him, and he shook his head. "Sierra, stop. We can't do this. You're injured."

"I'm okay," she said. "People with head injuries make out all the time."

He smiled faintly. "I don't think that's true."

"I'm good," she said. "Seriously."

He squeezed her hip. "You need to rest."

She sighed and slid off his lap, rubbing at the back of her neck before standing. "You're right."

She grabbed the remote and shut off the television. "I'll show you to the guest room."

He followed her up the stairs, deliberately keeping his gaze off her magnificent ass. His cock still strained at his jeans, and the temptation to ask Sierra if he could join her in her bed buzzed loudly in his brain.

"Here you go." Sierra swung open the door. "There are extra blankets in the closet if you get cold."

"I won't get cold," he said.

Her gaze drifted down his body, and he sucked in a breath when she stared at the prominent bulge at his crotch. "Sierra, you're killing me here."

"Sorry." She looked away, her cheeks turning pink. "Okay, well, goodnight."

"I'll check on you in a few hours. Are you okay with me coming in your bedroom?" he asked.

Her cheeks turned a darker pink, and she glanced at his dick again. He groaned when he realized what he'd inadvertently said. "To wake you up and check for signs of a concussion, I mean."

She avoided his gaze, staring at his chest instead. "Yes, that's fine."

There was an awkward silence, and he said, "Okay, well, good night."

"Good night, Everett." She turned and walked toward her bedroom, slipping inside and shutting the door gently behind her.

He sighed and refrained from smacking his hand against the door frame. Could he have fucked that up any worse?

CHAPTER 8

"So, you didn't have sex with him?" Hazel drank some wine. "Even though he spent the night and had an obvious erection?"

"No," Sierra said. "He woke me up twice in the night by shaking my foot, and he stood well away from the bed while he quizzed me on concussion symptoms. It was decidedly not sexy."

"He was trying to do the right thing," Indie said. "You had a head injury and shouldn't have been having sex."

"He was an amazing kisser," Sierra said.

"That's great, but he still made the right call," Indie said.

Sierra sighed. "Indiana, you know I love you, but I also kind of hate you right now."

Indie laughed. "I know. How awkward was the next morning?"

"So awkward." Sierra stared into her whiskey glass before draining the last two swallows. "He cleaned up the bathroom and packed away his tools in the truck while I was in the shower. I asked him if I could make him breakfast, and he declined so fast you'd have thought I'd asked if I could pull one of his teeth. We confirmed the dates for when he'll come back in the fall to work on the basement, and he left."

"Give it a few more days for your head to heal, and then text him," Hazel said. "Ask him if he wants to have dinner."

"I don't know if I should," Sierra said moodily. "He seriously couldn't leave my house fast enough Sunday morning."

She sighed and stretched out on the couch, staring at the spot where Everett had sat not three nights ago.

"He was obviously interested," Indie said. "And since when have you ever been shy about asking for what you want?"

"The worst that happens is he says no," Hazel said.

"Sure, but it's not like I never have to see him again if he rejects me. He'll be in my basement for two weeks."

"That's months from now," Hazel said. "Any awkwardness will be gone."

Sierra ran her fingers lightly across the sutures in her scalp. "Maybe I will. If he says no, it's not like I'll be in the basement with him while he works. I probably won't even see him because I'll be at work, right?"

"Right," Indie said. "And if he says yes…"

Indie wiggled her eyebrows and made a humping motion with her hips, making Sierra laugh. "I love how less of a prude you are now that you're fucking Val on a daily basis."

"I wasn't a prude before I met Val," Indie protested.

Sierra looked at Hazel, who shrugged. "You were a little bit of a prude."

"Fine," Indie said. "But I just want Sierra to have knock-your-socks-off sex like I am. It's called being a good friend.

Sierra laughed. "I appreciate that, but I'm not sure sleeping with my contractor is a good decision."

"Maybe not," Hazel said. "But sometimes bad decisions are exactly what a girl needs."

A slow grin spread across Sierra's face. "You make a valid argument, Hazel. I'll text him."

Indie cheered, and Hazel lifted her wine glass. "To making very bad decisions with very pretty men."

———

SIERRA SANK ONTO THE COUCH AND CLOSED HER EYES. SHE ghosted her fingers along her scalp, the thin ridge of a scar all that was left after her visit to the doctor today to remove the sutures.

She sipped at her whiskey, trying to will herself to get up and finish painting her bathroom. Hendrix and Val were coming by on Saturday morning to help her move the tub into the bathroom, which meant she needed to finish the painting and install the flooring in less than thirty-six hours.

Instead of getting up, she put her feet on the coffee table and drank another swallow of whiskey. It'd been a long and tiring day of work, just like the last ten days. She was decidedly happy that after tomorrow, she wouldn't have to step foot in the courtroom for two weeks, even if most of her holiday would be spent finishing the reno on the bathroom.

She sipped some more whiskey and grabbed her phone, scrolling to Everett's number in her text messages. Despite what she'd told Indie and Hazel last week, she hadn't called Everett. Partly nerves and partly because it'd been wild and woolly at work, culminating in twelve-hour work days and a real urge to toss some of the more slimy defense lawyers in contempt.

Text him. See if he wants to have dinner tomorrow night.

She studied the last text message from Everett. A perfectly polite message stating he'd received payment of her invoice and thanking her for her promptness. Nothing in it at all suggested he would enjoy seeing her again.

The worst that happens is he says no thanks.

She took a deep breath. She could do this. She wasn't some twenty-something girl who didn't know how to approach men. She was Sierra fucking Lewis, and any guy would be damn lucky to have her in his bed.

Her phone rang, scaring the shit out of her, and she dropped it on the floor. She muttered a curse and set her whiskey glass on the coffee table before scooping up her phone.

Her eyes widened. Holy shit. Everett was calling her.

She took a deep breath, smoothed her hair like an idiot, and hit the answer button. "Hi, Everett."

"Hi, Sierra. How are you?"

"I'm good. How are you?"

"Doing well," he said.

They were almost painfully formal, and she hated it. She'd had his tongue in her mouth, for fuck's sake.

"How's your head?" Everett asked.

"Good. Got the sutures out today, and it healed well," she said.

"I'm glad to hear it. So, I'm calling because I had a client cancel last minute today, which means I could finish your basement now instead of in the fall."

Was it dumb that disappointment was her strongest reaction? She should be thrilled that the basement would finished sooner than she thought. Instead, she was pouting that Everett wasn't calling to ask her out.

"Sierra? You still there?"

"Yes, sorry. I think the connection cut out for a minute," she lied.

"No problem," he said. "Would it work for you to have

me start on the basement now? I could start tomorrow afternoon."

"That would be perfect, actually," she said. "I'm on vacation for two weeks starting Monday, so I could use some of my holiday to paint the basement once you're finished."

"Great," he said. "I'll be there tomorrow then. Can you text me the new key code for the front door?"

"Oh, it's the same," she said.

She could hear the disapproval in his voice, even over the phone. "You should always change the key code after you've had a contractor in your home. Especially if they've been there long enough to know your routine."

She couldn't resist teasing him a little. "It's fine. I have a baseball bat by my bed and know some self-defense moves."

"I'm serious," he said. "Do you want to wake up in the middle of the night with some guy standing over your bed?"

"I guess it would depend on who the guy was," she said.

"Sierra," he said. She was pretty sure that the sound she could hear was his molars grinding together.

"Okay, okay, I'll change it once you've finished the basement," she said.

"Thank you," he said.

"Do you want to have dinner tomorrow night?" she asked. "I could order something or find a restaurant near my place."

His hesitation told her everything she needed to know.

"I can't," he said.

She told herself to let it go. If Everett wasn't into her anymore, he wasn't into her, but it wasn't in her damn nature to 'let things go'.

"Because you're not attracted to me anymore?" she asked.

He huffed out a dry laugh. "Trust me, that isn't it."

"Then why can't we have dinner together?"

"Because it wouldn't just be dinner. You'd invite me back

to your house after dinner. I'd accept because I think you're the hottest fucking woman I've ever met, and then we'd end up in bed. And I can't fuck a client, Sierra," he said bluntly.

"Whoa," she said, "who said I would fuck you after dinner?"

Embarrassment made him stutter. "I didn't… that is, I assumed…"

"Everyone knows you fuck *before* dinner," she said.

There was utter silence, and she burst into laughter. When she'd finally stopped giggling, Everett's way too sexy voice said, "If I were there right now, I'd spank your ass for that, Sierra."

Her breath caught in her throat, and her lady bits immediately woke the fuck up and waved a giant 'welcome to the party' sign at Everett.

Cool it, girl. He didn't mean anything by it. Just because spanking is your kink doesn't mean you should take an innocent comment and make it sexual.

"It would be worth it just to see the look on your face right now," she said, keeping her tone light. "Look, I understand wanting to keep things professional, but we're both adults, right? It's not like I'd fire you if we ended up being sexually incompatible or something. If we explore the attraction between us and it turns out not to be what we thought it would be, no big deal. We go back to the way it was."

"Unless one of us thinks it's good and the other doesn't. Then it's all kinds of awkward," he said. "No one likes being told they don't do it for someone."

"Fair," she said, "but we both seem emotionally mature enough to handle rejection."

He didn't say anything, and she said, "In the past, did you sleep with someone who hired you for a job, and it went badly?"

"No," he said. "I've never crossed that professional boundary. I've never been tempted to before now."

"I think it could be good between us," she said. "Don't you?"

He sighed. "I can't, Sierra. I'm sorry."

"Okay," she said. "I understand. I'll be at work tomorrow, but if you have any questions or need a refresher on what I want done in the basement, text me. I'm in court most of the day but have a few scheduled breaks."

"It should be fine," he said. "I have all of my notes from our initial consultation of the basement, but I'll reach out if I'm unclear."

"Great. Thanks again, Everett."

"You're welcome, Sierra."

She ended the call and spent five seconds acting like a fucking adult before she smacked her hand on the arm of the couch, let out a few choice profanities, and drained the rest of her whiskey.

She slumped back against the couch, staring at the ceiling as disappointment sat heavily on her chest. She didn't know why she felt so crushed by Everett's rejection, but she couldn't even pretend she was fine with it.

What if it wasn't just the client thing? What if he wasn't into her anymore, and that was just a convenient excuse?

So what if it is? You can't do anything about it. You've tried twice to start something with Everett, and he's repeatedly turned you down. Does the reason matter? Just take the L and move the fuck on.

She sighed and dragged her ass off the couch and up the stairs. She didn't have time to sulk over Everett's rejection. She had a bathroom to paint.

CHAPTER 9

"Hi, you're still here."

Everett smoothed the mud from his trowel onto the wall and then turned to face Sierra. "Hi, yes, sorry. I know it's late."

"Oh, it's fine," she said as she walked down the final few basement steps. "I just didn't expect you to work until eight on a Friday night."

"I got a late start," he said. "I was supposed to be finished by noon at my other job, but things went a little sideways, and I didn't finish until nearly three."

She stepped into the pool of light from the recessed lighting in the ceiling, and he studied her. She wore a navy blue pantsuit that fit her curves nicely, and her dark hair was pulled back in a smooth twist. She had on more makeup than he'd seen on her before, but not even the makeup could hide how exhausted she looked.

"Long day for you as well," he said.

She nodded. "Very."

"How often do you work this late?" he asked.

"Not that often, but the last day before vacation usually

brings out the chaos at work." She kept a healthy few feet between them, and the warmth of her smile was a little muted.

It was for the best that she kept her distance. He didn't trust that he wouldn't do something inappropriate like kiss her if she was within touching distance. He was determined to maintain his professionalism with her.

Yeah, because threatening to spank her was incredibly professional.

He cringed inwardly at the memory of what he'd said. It had popped out before he could stop it, but thank fucking Christ, she hadn't taken offense to the comment.

Maybe because she wants you to spank her?

He pushed that thought from his head immediately. Women like Sierra weren't into spanking. He dated women who had a soft and sweet vibe, almost always certain that they would be into a little domination in the bedroom.

Sierra might push every one of his buttons, but they wouldn't be sexually compatible. That was the real reason he'd rejected her. Well, that and because he was totally out of her league, and they both knew it. He might be the kind of guy Sierra would be willing to fuck, but it wouldn't go beyond that. She was a strong woman with a powerful and important career. She wouldn't want to be seen around town with a guy like him.

He realized he'd been staring at Sierra for nearly a minute.

"Sorry," he said. "Just thinking about… drywall stuff."

Fuck me sideways.

"That's fine," she said. "I'll let you get back to work."

She turned and headed up the stairs. He watched her perfect ass until it disappeared before slapping some more mud on the wall.

EVERETT STUCK HIS HEAD INTO THE KITCHEN. "SIERRA, I'M done for the day. I'll see you on…"

He trailed off, staring silently at the empty kitchen before heading down the hallway to the living room. It was also empty, and he hesitated at the stairs leading to the second floor. It was only nine, and he didn't think Sierra would be in bed already, but she had looked tired earlier.

So text her and go. You don't need to see her before you leave.

He didn't need to see her, but he wanted to see her.

He walked upstairs and headed toward her bedroom. Light spilled out from the half-opened door, and he knocked lightly on the door. "Sierra?"

"Come in," she called.

He stepped into her bedroom. Her bed had a roll of laminate underlayment on it, and Sierra crouched beside a box of laminate flooring, using an X-Acto knife to open the box.

She smiled at him. "Hey. Finished for the day?"

"Yes," he said. "What are you doing?"

She cocked an eyebrow at his admittedly stupid question. "Installing the flooring in the bathroom."

"It's nine o'clock at night," he said.

"I know." She flipped open the lid on the box and took out a piece of laminate.

"Are you some crazy night owl?" he asked.

She laughed tiredly. "Not in the least. In fact, I'm more of a morning person. But I didn't plan on working so late today, and Hendrix and Val are coming over in the morning to help me move the tub into the bathroom. I need to have the flooring installed before then."

"Can't you reschedule?" he asked.

"Not really. Tomorrow is the day that works best for both of them and since they're already doing me a huge favour, I don't want to ask for more," Sierra said.

She straightened and gave him a brief smile. "Have a good weekend, Everett. I'll see you on Monday."

Holding three pieces of flooring, she brushed past him. He followed her downstairs and down the hallway to the mudroom. She glanced at him, those little lines appearing between her eyebrows again. "Why are you following me?"

"Are you really going to install the flooring right now?" he asked. "You look exhausted."

"Such a charmer," she said, wrinkling her nose at him as she balanced the flooring in one hand and opened the garage door with the other.

She flicked on the light, and he stepped into the garage with her. A circular saw was already set up on a work table, and she set the flooring on the table before grabbing a pair of safety glasses.

"Sierra," he said, "wait a minute."

She sighed deeply and said, "Everett, I'm not trying to be rude, but I need to install this flooring. Can you lecture me on my poor time management skills on Monday?"

"That's not what I was going to say," he said. "I was going to ask if you wanted some help."

She blinked at him, surprise washing over her face. "What?"

"Do you want help?" he repeated. "I've installed laminate flooring before, and it will go a lot faster with the two of us."

"I'm sure you have better things to do on a Friday night than install flooring," she said.

"I don't," he said. "Unless going home and eating cold Chef Boyardee beefaroni straight from the can counts as Friday night plans."

A look of horror crossed her face. "Oh my God, tell me you don't eat that shit. It's nothing but chemicals."

"Tell me about it," he said. "But it's a guilty pleasure I indulge in once every few weeks."

"There are so many better guilty pleasures you could indulge in," she said.

He definitely could think of better ones. One in particular that involved a naked Sierra and his face buried between her firm thighs.

He cleared his throat. "Let me help you, Sierra."

"Are you sure?" she said.

"Positive," he said.

"In that case, let me show you where the knee pads are," she said with a grin.

"YOU HAVE TO ADMIT, WE MAKE A PRETTY GOOD FLOOR installation team," Everett said.

They'd ordered a pizza about two hours ago, and he was sitting on the floor, leaning against the wall and eating a cold slice.

Lying on her back on the newly installed bathroom floor, Sierra said, "We make a kick-ass floor installation team."

"This waterproof laminate is pretty nice." He studied the flooring. "I might pull up the old tile in my bathroom and put in some of this."

"Make sure you pay the extra for the quality stuff," Sierra said. "I'm in a Facebook group for home renovations, and this guy in the group cheaped out with the waterproof laminate in his bathroom and had many, many regrets when it bubbled and buckled after only a few months."

"Noted." Everett opened the pizza box and reached for

another slice. He paused with the slice near his mouth when she glanced at him. "What?"

"That's your fifth piece of pizza."

"I skipped lunch," he said. "Don't pizza slice shame me."

She laughed, watching as Everett took a giant bite. "I'm not. I'm just wondering if you have a hollow leg. Your body does not look like a body that consumes five slices of pizza at once. How often do you work out?"

"Honestly, not that much," he said. "I have a good metabolism. I jog several times a week, and the job keeps me fit."

Pretty fit was an understatement. Over the last four hours, she'd had plenty of opportunity to stare at Everett's body. She'd never thought she'd be turned on while installing flooring, but that was before Everett Caine walked into her life.

Everett finished the slice, then stretched one lean leg out and prodded her thigh with his foot. "You ready to finish the floor?"

"Nope," she said, staring at the ceiling again. "It's one in the morning, my back is killing me, and my knees feel like I've been giving blowjobs to an entire football team."

Everett laughed. "Lucky football team."

"You know it," she said. "I give excellent head."

"Everyone needs a talent," he said.

She turned her head to grin at him. "I am a woman of many, many talents, Everett Caine."

"I believe it," he said.

"It turned you on watching me lay that floor like a boss, didn't it?" she said.

"Fuck, yes."

That made her laugh, and she sat up, the laugh turning into a groan. She rubbed her aching lower back. "We have the flooring installed where the tub will go, and that's perfect. I'll finish off the rest tomorrow."

"It won't take long," he said. "Maybe another hour or so."

"I appreciate the enthusiasm, but Hendrix and Val will be here in eight hours, and I need at least five hours of sleep, a two-hour soak in the guest bathroom tub, and a shameful number of Advil if I'm gonna help them haul that tub in here."

She climbed to her feet, pretending she didn't feel every painful minute of the last four hours she'd been on her knees installing flooring. "Tomorrow night, when I'm soaking in my brand new tub, I will believe it was all worth it, but right now, I'm kicking myself for ordering such a big, heavy tub."

She held out her hand to Everett and helped tug him to his feet. He held her hand maybe a moment too long, enough to get her tired blood pumping through her veins, before dropping her hand and smiling at her. "Okay, I'll head home then."

He looked as tired as she felt, and for a moment, she considered offering the guest room to him to crash in. But after hitting on him twice and being rejected both times, the offer would make him think she was going for a three strikes and you're out scenario.

So, she nodded and said, "I appreciate your help tonight, Everett. Thank you."

"You're welcome," he said.

There was a brief awkwardness before he turned abruptly and left the bathroom. She followed him downstairs and watched silently as he slipped into his boots.

"Good night, Sierra." His gaze fell on her mouth.

"Night, Everett."

He continued to stare at her mouth. It was so quiet she could hear the clock ticking in the kitchen.

Kiss me, Everett. Please.

As if he heard her internal plea, he stepped closer and bent his head toward her. She rose on her tiptoes, swallowing her disappointment when he brushed his lips against her cheek.

He stepped outside, shutting the door behind him without looking back. Sierra slumped against the wall, her fingers brushing her cheek, the skin hot against her fingertips like she'd been branded.

CHAPTER 10

S ierra handed Val a coffee and pushed the box of pastries closer to Hendrix. "Help yourself, Hendrix."

"Thanks," Hendrix grabbed a pastry and bit into it as Val sipped his coffee.

"Thank you again, guys. I can't tell you how much I appreciate this," Sierra said.

"It's not a problem," Val said.

"You might think differently when we start moving that tub," Sierra said with a grin. "It's heavy as fuck."

"Just make sure you tell Hazel how strong I looked as I moved the tub," Hendrix said.

Sierra laughed. "I will be very complimentary."

Her doorbell rang, and she stood. "Excuse me, please."

She headed toward the front door, limping a little and rubbing at her lower back. She'd soaked in the tub this morning for over an hour and had a blisteringly hot shower afterward, but she could still feel the effects of being on her knees for so long last night.

Too bad all you got out of it was a bathroom floor.

She rolled her eyes as she opened the front door. Wishing her back and knees hurt because she'd spent the night blowing Everett was a foolish and -

"Everett? What are you doing here?" She couldn't hide her surprise.

"Hey." He gave her a cheerful grin and pushed past her. He certainly didn't walk like a man who'd spent an evening on his knees installing flooring.

He hung his jacket in the closet before raising an eyebrow. "Why are you looking at me like that?"

"I want to know what kind of witchcraft you're practicing."

"What do you mean?"

"I can barely move this morning, and you're hopping around as chipper as the fucking Easter Bunny."

He laughed. "I spend all day every day doing manual labour, Sierra. It'll take more than an evening of installing flooring to slow me down."

"Show off," she said, making him laugh again. "I thought you didn't work weekends? Is my basement drywalling that fascinating?"

"I'm here to help move the tub," he said.

He headed toward the kitchen, and Sierra followed him. "You're what?"

Everett grinned at Hendrix. "Hey, man, how are you?"

"Everett, hey, how's it going?" Hendrix said.

"Not bad." Everett held his hand out to Val. "Everett Caine."

"Val Jensen."

They shook hands, and Everett peeked into the pastry box. "Ooh, lemon danishes. May I?"

"Help yourself," Sierra said.

"You doing some drywalling this morning?" Hendrix asked.

"No. I'm here to help move the tub," Everett said. He bit into the Danish as Sierra poured a cup of coffee and handed it to him. "Thanks, Sierra."

"Great," Hendrix said. "Did you get my text about watching the game at my place this week?"

"Shit, yeah, sorry I forgot to reply. I'm in. I'll come by around seven Tuesday night," Everett said.

"Perfect. Turns out Val is a baseball fan as well, so he's joining us," Hendrix said. "I'm curious to see if Altuzo's batting average will be any better this season."

As the three men drank their coffee and discussed baseball stats like it was a matter of life and death, Sierra sipped her coffee and studied Everett. She liked how animated he got when they started talking about the latest game, and she liked the easy friendship between him and Hendrix. Gary didn't have friends. He saw other men in two lights - potential rivals or pawns he could use in the political world. It was nice to see Everett wasn't arrogant and insecure like Gary.

Hendrix ate the last bite of his pastry. "Sierra didn't invite us here this morning to eat her food and bore her with baseball, so what do you say we move a tub?"

Sierra laughed. "You're doing me a huge favour. If you want to eat pastries and talk baseball, that's perfectly fine with me."

Val glanced at his watch. "I have a meeting at the bike shop with a customer in about an hour, so we should get started."

Sierra followed them up the stairs, with Everett leading the way to her bedroom. In less than fifteen minutes, the three men moved the tub to its spot in the bathroom. She had to admit she was grateful Everett had shown up this morning. Her lower back hadn't been looking forward to lifting the tub.

They returned to the kitchen, and Sierra said, "Thank you again for your help."

"You're welcome. You sure you don't need me to stick around and help hook up the plumbing?" Hendrix asked.

"I'm good," she said. "I did the plumbing hookups for the guest bathroom without a problem, and I don't anticipate any issues with this one either."

"Okay," Hendrix said. "Everett, we'll see you Tuesday."

"You bet," Everett said.

Sierra walked Hendrix and Val to the front door and thanked them again before returning to the kitchen. Everett had helped himself to another Danish, and she poured them some fresh coffee.

"How did you sleep last night?" Everett asked.

"Like a rock," she said. "You?"

"Same," he said with a grin. "What are your plans for today?"

"Finishing the flooring and starting the tiling for the shower," she said.

"Did you buy this place before you and the mayor divorced or after?" he asked.

"After. Gary and I have been divorced for six years. I just bought this place a year and a half ago."

"What made you decide to buy a fixer-upper?" Everett leaned against the counter, sipping his coffee like he had nothing better to do than stand in her kitchen.

"It was always my dream," she said. "I tried doing it when Gary and I moved back here, but he was adamant that we buy a new home. He loathes doing renovations, and he refused to believe me when I said I would do them myself."

"Why?" Everett asked.

She shrugged. "Gary has old-fashioned views about a woman's place in the family. He was fine with me working before Michaela was born, but as soon as I gave birth, he suddenly wanted me to be a stay-at-home mom. I refused, and honestly, that was probably the beginning of the end of our marriage. We limped along for years after that, but things were never the same. He had this vision in his head of what our future looked like, and when I refused to go along with it like a good little Stepford Wife, he became a different person from the one I'd married."

She took a sip of hot coffee. "I couldn't wrap my head around this new version of Gary. We had talked about our future endlessly, for God's sake. He would go into politics. I would be a lawyer. We'd have one child, and I would continue working. It was all laid out neat as a fucking pin, you know?"

Everett nodded. "I get it."

"When we married, Gary didn't give a rat's ass if I went back to work or was a stay-at-home mom. He said whatever made me happy." She shook her head. "But he changed, and I changed too, and neither of us liked who the other person had become anymore."

"I think that happens a lot in marriages," Everett said. "Especially if you marry young."

"Which we did," Sierra said with a grimace. "Anyway, what about you? What's your divorce story?"

"Nothing exciting," he said. "We just grew apart."

He busied himself with closing the lid on the pastry box and returning the milk to the fridge. Sierra didn't get the sense that he had lied to her, but she was confident there was more to his divorce than he'd admitted.

She shrugged inwardly and finished the last of her coffee.

It wasn't her business, and they barely knew each other. He wasn't required to share his life story with her.

Everett turned back to face her, giving her an easy grin. "You ready?"

"Ready for what?" Her gaze drifted to his crotch before she could rein in her libido.

Everett cleared his throat. "I see you staring at my dick, Sierra."

She laughed and shrugged. "My bad, but I'd really like to get to know him better."

"It isn't because I don't want you," Everett said.

"I know," she said. "So, if it isn't a good dicking from you, what am I supposed to be ready for?"

He laughed so hard that coffee spilled out of his mug and landed on the floor with a wet splat. He grabbed some paper towels and cleaned it up before dropping the paper towels in the garbage. "For us to finish the flooring."

She stared at him. "You're helping me finish the flooring?"

"Yes," he said. "I need to see the job to the end, Sierra."

She laughed. "I appreciate your help, really, but I'm not asking you to spend your Saturday morning helping me install flooring."

"And tile a shower," he said. "And you didn't ask, I offered."

"Everett," she said, "you're not tiling my shower."

"Of course, I'm not," he said. "I've never tiled a shower before. But I'll stand there while you tile the shower and hand you tools and look pretty while I do it."

He put one hand on his hip and struck a pose, grinning when she started to laugh. "Oh my God, you're nuts."

"Certifiably," he said. "C'mon, that flooring won't finish installing itself."

"Are you sure?" she asked. "I'd love the company and the help, but I don't want you to waste your Saturday."

"It's not a waste," he said. "I want to help, Sierra. We're a kick-ass floor installation team, remember?"

She laughed and set down her coffee. "I remember. Let's do this then, flooring partner."

CHAPTER 11

"Sierra? Where are you?" Everett called from the hallway.

"Admiring the shower," she hollered.

He laughed and joined her in the bathroom. "It does look pretty damn great."

"Doesn't it?" she said. "I know I said this repeatedly while we were working on it, but I love this tile so much."

"Thank you for letting me use your guest shower again. I had no idea grouting could get so messy," Everett said.

"Was there even any hot water left? I took an extra long shower." Sierra glanced at Everett and then immediately looked away. Fuck, he was so sexy. After spending the last day and a half with him and realizing how funny and smart he was and how well they vibed, her desire for him only intensified. Why had she ever thought he was annoying? He wasn't. He was… great. And sexy as fuck, and it was killing her that she had to wait until he was finished in the basement to ask him out.

Again? You've asked him out twice, and he's repeatedly

turned you down. Take the hint, woman. He only wants to be your friend.

Sure, he wanted to be friends, but he'd also made it clear that he was attracted to her, so there was no harm in asking him out one more time once he was no longer her contractor. If he said no, she'd accept that there was more to it than just the contractor/customer thing and be happy with being his friend.

A friend who is endlessly horny for him.

Lord, wasn't that the truth.

She took a deep breath and faced him again. "What would you like for dinner? I'm ordering in because I'm way too tired to cook."

"You don't have to buy me dinner, Sierra," he said.

"Are you kidding me?" she said. "You spent your entire Saturday helping me with house renovations. Of course I'm buying you dinner. Hell, I should buy you dinner every night this week."

He laughed. "I didn't volunteer to help because I was looking for free dinners."

"I know." She smiled at him.

He took a step closer. He smelled like her body wash, and while that shouldn't have been a turn-on, her body reacted like it was. Her breasts felt full and achy, and her pussy throbbed pleasantly.

"How is your head, by the way? I kept meaning to ask if you were getting any headaches or dizziness." His voice was a sexy rasp, and when he reached out and threaded his fingers into her hair, she lost all ability to think.

Wordlessly, she stepped closer and bent her head, resting her forehead against his chest as his fingers combed gently through her hair before he traced his fingertips across the scar.

Her hands shaking, she latched onto his hips, her fingers digging into the denim when he retraced the scar. "It feels fine. No headaches or dizziness."

"The scar is hardly noticeable," he said.

She lifted her head, her response dying in her throat when she saw the lust in his gaze. He sucked in a harsh breath, his nostrils flaring. "I want you so much, Sierra."

"I want you too," she whispered.

They studied each other for a few seconds before she said, "I know you have reservations about fucking a customer, and I know we had a rough start when we first met, but we have amazing chemistry. I think we're both mature enough to deal with any potential fallout from sleeping together without affecting your contract work. Don't you agree?"

"Yes," he said.

She waited, and when he said nothing else, she said, "Is it just your rule about fucking a customer that's stopping you?"

He hesitated. "No. Despite our attraction and chemistry, I know we won't be compatible in bed."

"Why do you think that?" she asked.

He tried to step away, and she tightened her grip on his hips. "Tell me, Everett."

"I'm not vanilla when it comes to sex," he said. "I like certain things in the bedroom that you will not. I might be able to give you vanilla sex once or twice, but I know myself, and it won't stay vanilla for long."

"Intriguing," she said with a small smile. "I'm not exactly vanilla myself."

"We still won't be compatible, Sierra. Trust me."

"Why don't you tell me what you like in bed and give me a say in the matter," she said.

"Control," he said bluntly. "Control, and spanking, and

sex that's on the rougher side. So, you can see why it won't work between us."

This time, when he pulled away, she let him go. He paused in the doorway, gripping the frame tightly as he stared at the newly installed tub. "I thought I could spend time with you as a friend without wanting to fuck you, but I was wrong. I'll keep things professional between us from now on. I'll see you on Monday."

"Everett, wait," she said. "Aren't you going to ask me what my kink is?"

He hesitated, indecision and curiosity warring on his face before the curiosity won out. "What's your kink?"

"Being spanked. Being bossed around in the bedroom, and," she joined him in the doorway, resting one hand against his chest, "I definitely wouldn't say no to being manhandled a bit in bed."

His mouth dropped open, and she couldn't help but giggle. "Oh my God, your face."

"Sierra, I… wait… are you serious?" he said.

"So serious," she said. "And honestly, you shouldn't be this surprised. My stressful job requires me to make life-altering decisions, and I'm an obvious control freak outside of the bedroom. It's practically the world's biggest cliche that I want to give up control in the bedroom."

"It's been my experience since my divorce that women who are the take charge type are like that in the bedroom," he said.

"I'm not." She wrapped her arms around his waist and kissed his chest through his t-shirt. "Your flavour of kink is my flavour, too, Everett Caine. So, why don't we have some dinner, and then you can take me to bed and cover my ass with your handprints like I've been fantasizing about since the first moment I saw you in Home Depot."

"No," he said.

Disappointment as heavy as her new tub dropped onto her. She let go of Everett, but before she could step away, his arm slid around her waist, and he pulled her up tight against his body. His sexy grin made every muscle in her lower belly twinge with anticipation.

"Everyone knows you fuck *before* dinner, Sierra."

———

SIERRA OPENED HER NIGHTSTAND DRAWER AND BROUGHT OUT a condom and the lube. She set both on her nightstand before kicking off her shoes. The last few times she'd had sex, the lube had been a requirement, but whether she wasn't getting wet enough because of her aging body or because of her partner, she wasn't sure.

She turned to face Everett. He'd already removed his shoes and socks and was in the process of removing his shirt. She stared at his upper body. He had a well-defined chest covered in a light layer of salt and pepper chest hair and a flat stomach that wasn't a six-pack. She liked that he didn't have one. Liked that his body wasn't a perfect specimen of smooth skin and hard muscle. It made her feel less self-conscious about her muffin top and other imperfections.

Everett tossed his shirt aside before studying her. "Come to me, Sierra."

His voice had changed. She'd always found it sexy, but now… one simple command from him in *that* voice and her panties were a soaking mess.

Won't be needing that lube tonight, sweetheart.

Fucking right she wouldn't.

She joined him at the end of the bed, stopping about half a foot away when he held out his hand. He looked her up and down before his gaze focused on her tits. "Strip for me."

She tugged her shirt over her head without hesitation and shoved her yoga pants down her legs, stepping out of them and kicking them aside before pulling off her socks. She unhooked her bra and let it slide down her body, her stomach clenching tight at the look of appreciation on Everett's face when he saw her naked breasts.

She hesitated at removing her panties, and Everett's voice turned stern. "All of it, Sierra."

She hooked her thumbs in the waistband and pulled them down her legs, stepping out of them. Everett studied her pussy before smiling at her. "Stand nice and straight for me with your hands behind your back."

Her heart thumping, her nipples hard as glass, and her pussy leaking like a fucking faucet, she did what he asked. Everett stepped closer and studied her breasts for long moments. She wanted to squirm but didn't.

Finally, he traced a circle around her left nipple and then her right, making her moan quietly.

"Very nice," he said before moving behind her. His hand cupped one ass cheek and squeezed, and she moaned again when he pressed against her. His jeans were rough against her skin, and she could feel his erection.

He tugged her hands apart and moved her arms to her sides before he slid his arms around her and cupped her tits. He kissed her neck, his hands kneading her breasts.

"Such pretty little breasts, Sierra," he whispered into her ear before plucking at her nipples.

She cried out, her back arching and her hands reaching behind her to grab onto his thighs.

"Sensitive," he said approvingly before flicking her

nipples. She dug her fingers into his thighs, biting her bottom lip when he pinched them hard.

"Good," he said before kissing her throat again. "Give me a safe word, Sierra."

"Red," she said. "Yellow to slow down."

"Red is your safe word," he said to confirm, "and yellow means you want to slow down."

She nodded, and he licked a path to her earlobe before sucking on it. She squirmed against him when he stroked her lower belly and toyed with the small patch of pubic hair at the top of her sex.

She parted her legs wide, but he didn't move lower, instead touching the small scar at the top of her belly button. "What's this from?"

"A belly button ring that got infected," she said, her voice breathless. "Everett, touch me, please."

"No," he said and that one softly spoken word sent her lust soaring.

He slid his hands down her arms. "Turn around, Sierra."

She turned to face him, and he smoothed her hair back from her face. "You're going to suck my dick now. If you do a good job, I'll reward you with a pussy eating. Does that sound fair?"

"Yes, Everett," she said.

He snagged a pillow from her bed and dropped it at his feet. He raised an eyebrow at her when she didn't move, and, her face flushing, she knelt on the pillow in front of him.

"Good," he said. "Now, do what I've told you to do."

CHAPTER 12

E verett could barely stop his hips from jutting forward when Sierra unbuttoned and unzipped his jeans. Jesus, he was already on the edge of his control, and she hadn't even sucked him off yet.

But her perfect body, how quickly she gave him her submission, and her response to his touch, had every part of him aching to bury his cock deep in her pussy.

Instead, he kept his need under wraps with iron control as she tugged his jeans and briefs down his legs. He stepped out of them, and she tossed them aside before straightening. Her warm breath washed over his aching dick. He wasn't anything special in size, clocking in at just over average for both length and thickness, but the hungry way Sierra eyed his dick made it very difficult not to shove his entire dick past her pretty pink lips.

Instead, he gripped the shaft and gave it a few slow strokes until precum coated the head. He rubbed the head against Sierra's lips, humming his approval when she licked her lips clean.

"Yummy," she said with a cute grin.

He laughed and threaded his hands in her hair, mindful of the scar, even though she'd said it didn't hurt. He gathered her hair into a loose ponytail and tugged her head back.

"I won't eat your pussy if you don't please me on your knees, Sierra. Do you understand?"

"Yes, Everett," she said. "Wait, do you want me to call you sir?"

He shook his head. "Not necessary unless it's a kink for you?"

"No," she said.

He used his free hand to rub his thumb over her lower lip. He hadn't even kissed her yet, but that was deliberate. Kissing her before had nearly knocked him on his ass, and he needed to keep his wits about him. Especially since this was their only night together. Sierra was using him to satisfy an itch, and while he was okay with that, he still needed to protect his heart.

Sierra's soft hands stroked his bare thighs. "Hey, everything okay?"

He made himself focus on her and the pleasure they were about to give each other. "Yes. If you need me to stop and your mouth is full, tap me three times on the thigh. Understand?"

"Yes," she said.

He tugged on her hair again, and she leaned forward, parting her pink lips. He bit back his groan when she used her tongue to lick around the sensitive ridge before investigating the slit at the head. Fresh precum spurted out, and she licked it away eagerly as she wrapped her hand around his base and squeezed lightly.

She slid her mouth down over his cock, and he released his breath in a harsh hiss, his hand tightening in her hair. He watched for nearly five minutes as she licked and sucked and explored his cock with a single-minded determinedness that he found incredibly sexy.

He wasn't surprised at how good she was at sucking his dick. Sierra wanted to be the best at anything she did, whether installing laminate, tiling a shower, or sucking his dick.

She took one of his balls into her mouth, sucking lightly, and he groaned, his hand gripping her hair hard.

She released him and leaned back, a self-satisfied smile on her face. "Finally, a reaction. I'm really worried I'm not going to get that pussy eating."

He smiled and rubbed her now swollen bottom lip. "You're doing very well, Sierra. Keep going."

She stared up at him, those pretty dark eyes full of need, before she nodded and sucked his cock again. He watched her cheeks hollow as she sucked hard, and he groaned again before he gripped her hair in both hands and pulled her off with a soft pop.

She licked her lips, staring up at him. "What's wrong?"

"Open," he said hoarsely. "Open so I can fuck your pretty mouth."

She opened her mouth immediately, and a fresh wave of lust washed over him at her obedience.

"Remember, three taps, baby," he said before he shoved his cock between her lips. He fucked her mouth roughly, using her hair to hold her still as he pumped himself in and out of her mouth.

She gripped his thighs, keeping her gaze on his face as he used her mouth. When he slipped down her throat, and his entire cock was enveloped in her hot mouth, he moaned loudly. He palmed the back of her head, keeping her pressed against him until she squeezed his thighs. He released her, letting her pull back to draw in some oxygen. He wiped off the combination of spittle and precum on her chin before sliding his cock into her mouth again. He made her deep-throat him repeatedly until he was on the verge of his orgasm, and her lips were swollen, and her eyes watered uncontrollably.

He pulled out, gripping the base of his dick to stop from just nutting all over Sierra's beautiful breasts. She gasped for air, her chest heaving, and wiped at her mouth.

"You are so fucking beautiful," he said and lifted her to her feet.

He pushed her onto her back on the bed and shoved her legs apart before bending down and licking from her opening to the top of her slit.

Sierra cried out, her hips bucking forward and her hands grabbing the sheet below her.

"You were so good at sucking my dick," he crooned, stretching out between her legs. "I'm going to eat your pretty pussy until you come all over my face."

He spread her wet pussy lips with his thumbs and licked his lips at the sight of her swollen pink clit.

"Perfect," he whispered before licking it with a broad, flat stroke of his tongue.

SIERRA'S JAW ACHED, AND HER KNEES HURT, BUT THE PAIN magically disappeared when Everett licked her clit.

She shrieked and clutched at his head, trying to shove his face into her pussy. He laughed and grabbed her hands, holding them against her thighs as he stared up at him. "When did you have your pussy eaten last?"

"It's been a while," she panted. "So, you should get back to it."

He grinned. "You aren't trying to tell me what to do, are you?"

"No," she said, "but you promised, Everett."

"If you did a good job sucking my cock," he said.

"I did a fucking amazing job," she said before smacking him in the butt with her foot.

He laughed again. "Yeah, baby, you did."

He made another long lick from her opening to her clit, and she let her legs fall wide. Everett didn't release her wrists as he licked and sucked at her clit, and she pulled lightly, her desire going to a whole new level when he tightened his grip.

She panted and moaned, her body quivering as Everett explored her pussy with his tongue. He was thorough, leaving nothing overlooked as he licked and nibbled at her pussy lips, stiffened his tongue and slid it into her opening, and then returned to her clit to lick and suck.

She could hear herself moaning and pleading breathlessly as Everett teased her with every stroke of his tongue. He lifted his head slightly, studying her pussy and muttering, "Such a pretty, tasty little cunt," before diving back in.

She shrieked when he sucked hard on her clit, and her orgasm, intense and completely unexpected, washed over her. She bucked against his hands and mouth, the pleasure moving through her body like lightning until she collapsed against the bed, trembling wildly.

Everett sat up and wiped his face on the sheet before he reached for the condom. She sucked in harsh breaths of oxygen as Everett rolled on the condom and patted her hip. "On your hands and knees, Sierra."

She rolled to her stomach but stayed there. Her body was weak, and she needed to recover from her orgasm.

"Hands and knees," Everett repeated.

"Need a couple of minutes," she mumbled.

The slap to her ass was sharp and painful and made her cry out. Everett spanked her again, the sound of his hard hand against her soft ass echoing in the room.

"Do as I say, Sierra," Everett said, his voice sharp.

She scrambled to her hands and knees, her ass stinging and her arms trembling as she tried to lock them into place so she didn't fall on her face on the bed.

"Everett," she said, "I'm sorry, I -"

He spanked her again, and oh, fuck, it hurt so bad, but under that hurt was... bliss.

She stopped talking and lowered her upper body to the bed, resting her hot cheek against the bed and spreading her legs wide for Everett.

"Better," he said. The approval in his voice sent a hot flush of happiness through her entire body.

He reached for a pillow and grabbed her hair with one hand, pulling her up as he shoved a pillow under her upper body. His movements were quick and rough as he arranged her how he wanted her. He didn't speak to her or give her soft touches of reassurance. She'd had her pleasure, and now he would use her body to take his.

Her stomach clenched, and her pussy tightened with need at the thought. Everett, his dick pressed against her entrance and ready to take her, grunted in annoyance at how her body tried to keep him out and spanked her hard. "Don't even think of denying me your little pussy, Sierra."

"I'm not," she gasped out. "I just... I need a minute."

He reached between her legs and rubbed her clit hard, his fingers so rough against the sensitive flesh that it bordered on pain. He coated his fingers with her cream and pushed two into her tight channel.

She clenched around him, and he groaned before fucking

her hard with his fingers. She cried out when he squeezed her sore ass with his free hand.

"You will take my dick, Sierra," he said. He pulled his fingers free and pushed them into her mouth. "Suck."

She cleaned away her taste from his fingers as he lined his dick up at her entrance again. He reached under her and tweaked her nipples with his wet fingers as he pushed fully into her.

She cried out and arched her back against the delicious burn of his invasion, clenching around him when he slapped her ass again.

He groaned. "Fuck! Honey, don't do that."

"Can't help it," she panted.

He growled his disapproval before gripping her hips and pounding into her. She grabbed the sheets and buried her face in them, moaning and crying out as fresh pleasure permeated her body.

Everett fucked her harder, his fingers sinking into her flesh. She lifted her head and moaned his name as her second orgasm washed over her. Her pussy gripped him tight, and Everett cursed loudly before he drove deep a final time.

Wet warmth flooded her pussy, and their bodies shook and swayed. When Everett finally pulled out, she collapsed on her face, wondering at the muttered curse he made. She could hear Everett leave the bedroom, and she rolled to her back, breathing hard.

He returned a few minutes later, the condom gone and a wet washcloth in his hand. He sat on the bed beside Sierra and pressed the warm washcloth between her legs, cleaning her with studious concentration.

When he was finished, he said, "The condom broke."

"Oh," she said.

He tossed the washcloth in the hamper. "Sorry."

"Not your fault," she said. She sat up, hugging her knees to her chest.

"I've had a vasectomy," he said.

She grinned. "Yeah, that's not a concern. I went into menopause in my early forties."

"Okay," he said. "I'm infection free, but I'll show you my records."

"Same here," she said, "but I'm happy to share my medical results."

They studied each other before Everett said, "Should I go?"

"You just gave me a crazy good orgasm, and the first thing you ask is if you should go? Buddy, I might chain you up in my basement. Of course, only after you finish drywalling it."

He laughed. "Of course."

She cupped his face. "I still owe you dinner, and I'd like you to stay the night, but there's no pressure."

She paused. "About staying the night. You are required to eat dinner with me. We used up a lot of energy, and I will not be responsible for you being so weak from the amazing sex and lack of calories you get in a car crash driving home."

"That's fair," he said.

She smiled again before rubbing his cheekbone with her thumb. "It was pretty fucking good between us, wasn't it?"

"Yes," he said. "The best I've had."

She couldn't help her pleased smile. "Me too. Does that mean you'll stay the night with me, Everett Caine?"

"Yes," he said. "There's nothing I want more."

CHAPTER 13

"Y ou ready to tell me what's wrong yet?" Hendrix rested his golf club on the ground and watched as Everett lined up his shot and swung the club.

The small white ball arced to the left, and Everett swore loudly when it landed in the wooded area. "Why do you think something's wrong?"

Hendrix followed him back to the golf cart, and they loaded their clubs into the golf bags before climbing into the cart. "Maybe because when you found out I was going golfing this afternoon, you asked if you could join me."

He started the cart, and Everett gripped the handhold as Hendrix drove. "I thought it would be a fun way to spend a Sunday afternoon with a friend."

Hendrix laughed. "Bullshit. You hate golfing, Everett. So, tell me what's wrong."

He stopped the cart next to the wooded area, and Everett stared at the lush green course in front of them. "I slept with Sierra last night."

"Shocking," Hendrix said dryly.

"What does that mean?" Everett said.

"It means you were eye-banging each other in the kitchen with Val and me there. I knew the minute you were alone, you'd fuck her," Hendrix said. "Tell me you at least let her hook up the new tub before you banged her."

Everett rolled his eyes. "We installed the new tub, finished the flooring, and did the shower tiling before we had sex."

"Damn," Hendrix said. "And you still had the energy to have sex afterward? I'm impressed."

"Look, just because you're too old to satisfy your woman properly -"

"Hazel has no complaints, thank you very much," Hendrix laughed. "I'm just saying, you've got a lot of stamina for an old guy."

"Thanks," Everett said.

Hendrix studied him. "So, it didn't go well then? Sierra wasn't into your... tastes."

"It was incredible," Everett said. "We're, uh, compatible in bed."

"Then why are you making yourself miserable by golfing with me this afternoon?"

"She asked me to spend the night," Everett said. "I did, but I woke up alone this morning. She'd left me a note and said she didn't want to wake me, but she'd gotten an early morning text from her kid and needed to leave."

He stared at the distant figures of a couple of golfers at the hole ahead. "I think she might have regretted last night and made up an excuse."

"She didn't," Hendrix said. "She called Hazel this morning. Michaela was in a car accident."

"Holy shit," Everett said, his self-pity disappearing immediately. "Is she okay?"

"Yes. Apparently, it was a fender bender, but Michaela was pretty shaken by it, so Sierra drove up to see her."

Everett took his phone out, scrolling to Sierra's number. He started to text her and then stopped and erased it, tucking his phone back into his pocket.

"You aren't going to text her?" Hendrix asked.

He shook his head. "No. She obviously didn't want me to know, or she would have woken me. Last night was about sex for her and nothing more."

"You don't know that for sure," Hendrix said.

"I do," Everett said. "Women like her only want one thing from men like me."

"You keep saying that, but maybe you should actually talk to Sierra about it," Hendrix said.

"I don't have to," Everett said. "I know it's true."

"Fuck, Wendy really screwed with your head, man," Hendrix said.

"No, she showed me the truth, and I'm grateful for it." Everett climbed out of the golf cart, grabbed a club, and trudged into the woods.

Sierra let herself into the house, kicking the door shut with her foot and dropping her keys and purse on the side table in the hallway. She headed toward the kitchen and set the bag of food on the table.

She was exhausted, she had a headache, and she was pretty sure her jaw hadn't unclenched the entire drive home from Michaela's. She had enough tension in her body to fuel a jet plane. But that's what happened when she spent over twenty-four hours with Gary.

Still, despite how tired she was, her excitement at seeing

Everett's work truck in her driveway had given her a boost. It was weird and a little disconcerting how much she'd missed him, but she wouldn't focus on that. She would focus on…

"Holy shit." She stared at the wall where she'd hung her cookbook shelf. When she'd left on Sunday morning, the two holes from her disastrous attempt at shelf hanging had still been there. Now, they were patched and mudded with fresh drywall.

"Welcome back." Everett's low voice came from behind her.

She turned, barely able to control her inappropriate urge to fling her arms around him as if she'd just returned from war.

"Hi, Everett. Thank you for doing that." She pointed to the wall.

"You're welcome. I'll sand it tomorrow, and then we can repaint and hang the shelf. I've got some molly bolts in my tool case."

She liked how he said 'we'. Liked pretending that it meant something more than it did.

"That sounds good," she said.

"How are you?" He studied her with those pretty hazel eyes that didn't miss a thing.

"Good," she lied. "A little tired."

"How is Michaela?" he asked. "I saw Hendrix on Sunday, and he told me what happened."

"She's okay. She went to the urgent care to be safe, but everything checked out. It was just a fender bender, but it was her first car accident, and the guy who ran into her was a real dick on the scene. Tried to convince her that it was her fault and that they didn't need to exchange insurance and could take care of it privately."

"What an asshole," Everett said.

"He really was. Luckily, she stayed firm on getting his insurance information, but it was still traumatizing for her."

"I'm sorry that happened to her," Everett said.

"How are you?" she asked.

"Fine. I'm finished for the day and have the second room's walls up and mudded."

"That's awesome," she said.

She hated the sudden awkwardness between them. She'd spent most of yesterday thinking about Everett and how good it would feel to see him again, and now it felt like they were strangers.

"Okay, well, I should go," Everett said.

Weird panic fluttering at her edges, she said, "Do you want to stay for dinner? I picked up some takeout. It's just soup, but there's plenty."

He hesitated before shaking his head. "I have to go."

Bitter disappointment burrowed into her chest. The tension and the stress of the last day and a half dropped onto her shoulders like a small tank, and she was horrified to realize she was on the verge of tears.

She quickly turned away from Everett, gripping the sink hard and staring blankly out the kitchen window. "Sure, okay. Have a good night. I'll see you tomorrow."

She definitely sounded like she was about to cry, and she hoped like hell that Everett left before she started sobbing.

She jumped when Everett's warm hand rested against her lower back. "You okay?"

"Fine," she said. "See you tomorrow."

"You don't sound fine," he said.

She sighed. "I appreciate the concern, but could you go? Because I'm about to cry, and the only thing worse than crying is crying in front of you."

She tried half-heartedly to resist when Everett turned her

around but gave up at his hands' gentle but firm pressure. She was mortified when a tear slipped down her cheek, but Everett brushed it away gently.

"It's okay to cry in front of me, Sierra."

"No, it isn't," she said.

He pressed his lips against her forehead. "Yes, it is."

More tears slid down her cheeks, and when Everett pulled her into his embrace, she buried her face in his throat and breathed him in. He rubbed her back and didn't say anything. Just let her cling to him until she was back in control.

She leaned back and smiled at him. Everett frowned. "Shit, I got you covered in drywall dust."

She studied the white on her t-shirt. "I don't care."

He smoothed his thumb across her cheekbone, and as much as she wanted to beg him to stay, she stepped away from him instead. "Thanks, Everett. I'll see you tomorrow?"

He took her hand and tugged her toward the stairs. "Come with me, Sierra."

"You have to go, you said." Sierra climbed the stairs behind him. "Everett, I don't want you staying out of pity because I cried, okay?"

"I'm not," he said. "I want to stay."

She made him stop outside of her bedroom, studying his face intently. "Do you?"

"Yes," he said without hesitating.

They stepped into her bedroom, but he took her hands when she reached to take off his t-shirt.

"What's wrong?" she asked. "I thought we were having sex?"

She trailed after him when he walked into her bathroom to her new soaker tub. He started the water before returning to her and tugging off her shirt.

"Sex in a tub. I like it," she said.

He smiled and shook his head. "You're going to have a soak in the tub alone, Sierra."

"I'd rather have you join me," she said.

"You're exhausted," he said. "You don't need to be fucked right now."

"How will we know if we don't try?" she said.

He laughed and tugged down her leggings. "No, Sierra. You need a hot soak, warm soup, and sleep."

"You're no fun," she said, even though she knew everything Everett said was true. She was exhausted, and as much as she enjoyed fucking him, the idea of a hot bath and sleep was nearly as intoxicating.

He stripped off the rest of her clothes and turned the water off, testing the temperature before tugging her toward the tub. "Climb in. I'll come check on you in a bit."

She sunk into the hot water with a sigh of contentment. "Thank you, Everett."

"You're welcome, Sierra."

"Are you still awake?" Everett's low voice washed over her.

"Mostly," she said. She'd actually been on the verge of dozing off.

She forced her eyelids open. Everett had brought the small stool from the kitchen that she used to reach the top shelves of the cupboards, and he placed it beside the tub before sitting on it. He had changed into a fresh shirt and held a wine glass in his hand.

"You getting hungry?" he asked.

"A little," she said. "You ready to join me in the tub?"

He grinned. "Be good, Sierra."

"Where's the fun in that?"

She sat up and reached for his wine glass. He handed it over, and she drank a few swallows. "Should I have woken you when I left Sunday morning? I didn't know if leaving the note was the right decision."

"It's all good," he said.

She returned his wine glass to him and rested her arms on the side of the tub. "Can I ask you a question?"

"Sure."

"Do you think I'm bad at kissing?"

His face turned a soft red. "No, why?"

"You haven't kissed me since that night on the couch," she said. "And I don't know if it's because you think I'm a terrible kisser or if you're just not into kissing, but kissing is important to me, and -

He leaned over the tub and kissed her. He slid his tongue into her mouth when she parted her lips, and she returned his kiss eagerly. When he pulled back, she was breathless, and he had a noticeable erection.

"You really should get in the tub with me," she said.

She leaned back and cupped her breasts, playing with her nipples as Everett watched with a hungry look. She slid her hand down her body and cupped her mound, rubbing lightly at her clit.

"Fuck, Sierra," he said.

"That's exactly what I want," she said.

He leaned over the tub and kissed her again, dipping his hand into the water to cup and squeeze her breasts. She sucked on his tongue, delighting in the soft groan he made. He pulled at her nipples, pinching them lightly and sending a line of fire straight to her pussy.

She rubbed harder at her clit. She forgot about her

exhaustion and her growling tummy. She wanted to come, wanted to feel Everett deep inside of her again.

"Everett, please," she panted against his mouth. "Fuck me."

He slid his hand down her stomach and pushed her hand out of the way. His rough fingers rubbed her clit, and she cried out, her back arching and sending a wave of water dangerously close to splashing over the tub.

Everett rubbed her clit in fast and firm circles. She gripped his arm, gasping when he took her mouth in a hard deep kiss that sent a surge of wetness to her pussy.

She rocked her hips against his hand, her orgasm already close and her body nearly begging for release.

"Everett," she whimpered. "Oh God, Everett, I…"

"Give it to me, Sierra," he demanded. "Give me your orgasm right now."

She moaned, her hips jerking and twisting as she climaxed against Everett's hand. He swallowed her cries of pleasure, kissing her repeatedly as she came down from the high of her orgasm.

She slumped against the back of the tub, panting loudly and her body quivering. "God, that was so good."

Everett grinned and squeezed her thigh before standing and reaching for the towel. "C'mon, sweetheart, it's time to get out of the tub."

CHAPTER 14

Sierra stood, feeling wobbly in the knees and even more tired than before. She yawned and held onto Everett for support as she climbed out of the tub, and he wrapped her in a towel.

He pressed a kiss against her mouth and led her to the bedroom, pulling back the covers and urging her to climb in. She did, and he propped a pillow between her back and the headboard.

"I'll be right back," he said.

She blinked at him in confusion. Wasn't this when he was supposed to fuck her? Before she could ask, he was gone.

She yawned again and grabbed her phone from the nightstand. Michaela had texted her, and she quickly replied as Everett returned to the bedroom.

He had a tray with two bowls on it, and she could smell the delicious scent of pho drifting from them. Everett set the tray on her lap and stripped to his boxer briefs before carefully climbing in beside her.

She smiled at him and handed him his bowl. "Thank you. I hope you like pho."

"Love it," he said.

Her stomach growled, and he nudged her with his elbow. "Eat, Sierra."

They ate in silence. Sierra's hunger had roared back to life, and she was too busy stuffing delicious noodles into her mouth to think of making conversation.

When they were finished, Everett took the bowls to the kitchen and returned with water for both of them. She drank half her glass and set it on her nightstand. Everett sat beside her with the covers pulled to his waist and one big hand resting on her thigh.

"Thank you, Everett," she said.

"You're welcome. Are you ready to tell me what's wrong?" he asked.

"Wouldn't you rather I give you a blow job?" she said, tracing one finger over his groin.

He smiled and took her hand, kissing the palm of it. "Getting a blow job from you is my new favourite thing, but I'd like to know what has upset you. I have a feeling it's more than just Michaela being in a fender bender."

She sighed and took another drink of water. "Gary showed up to support Michaela. He was the shittiest of husbands, but I won't try to pretend that he isn't a good dad. He's an amazing dad, actually. He and Michaela are very close, and he loves her with everything in him."

"Michaela's lucky to have two supportive parents," Everett said.

"Three, actually. Gary's new wife, Roxanne, is also amazing with her. Loves her like she's her own. I'm not surprised. Michaela's an amazing kid, she really is, and I'm not being biased because I'm her mom. Because trust me, she isn't without her faults either, but overall, she's incredible.

Thoughtful and kind but knows what she wants and who she is and doesn't let anyone push her around."

Everett smiled. "So, a lot like her mom then."

"When I decided to leave Gary, it devastated Michaela. I promised her we'd always be a family, and I've kept that promise. We spend almost every holiday together, and Gary and I are always civil to each other in her presence."

"Does she know how Gary treated you when you were married?" Everett asked.

"She knows we fought a lot. We tried to keep it quiet, but kids are smart. They know when their parents are fighting. She doesn't know how disrespectful he became, how he tried to dictate my life and demand that I give up my dreams to support his."

Sierra pulled at a loose thread on the bed cover. "I don't want her to know those things. I know Gary has made some subtle jabs at me to Michaela, but for the most part, it hasn't affected her and my relationship, so I've let it go. She blames me for the divorce, and while that hurts, I'd rather take the blame than have her entire world rocked by discovering her dad's true nature."

"That's not fair to you, though," Everett said.

She shrugged. "Life isn't always fair, you know? Besides, despite that, I have a great relationship with Michaela, and I can handle a little blame. What matters is she's happy and loves her parents and knows she can come to us for support in anything."

"So, was Gary a dick while you were there with Michaela?" Everett asked.

"Such a dick," she said. "He hates that I bought an old house to restore."

"Why does he care?" Everett asked.

"A couple of reasons. He thinks I'm sinking too much

money into it, and I won't have enough to cover my share of Michaela's tuition. It isn't true, by the way, but he refuses to stop nagging me about it. You should have heard how furious he was when I hired you to do the drywalling." She laughed. "I told him I would do the renovation myself, but he calls me a liar because I needed to bring in a plumber and an electrician last year and now a drywaller this year. He can't comprehend that there are some home renovations an average person can't or shouldn't do on their own."

"Jesus, he's an idiot," Everett said.

"Yes, he is," Sierra said. "The second reason is that image is very important to him, and he thinks his ex-wife living in a "rundown shithole," as he calls it, reflects poorly on him. He's such a fucking snob, and it infuriates me. He looks down on everyone who doesn't make six figures a year."

"He sounds great," Everett said dryly.

She laughed. "Yeah, he's a real peach. His public persona as mayor is so different from who he is. It's scary how much of a chameleon he can be. Anyway, whenever Michaela wasn't with us, he wouldn't stop snipping at me about everything and anything I'd done that pissed him off in the last, oh… twenty-five years. It got really old, really fast, and it was basically thirty-six hours of me holding in my temper. Which, I don't know if you've noticed, is a real struggle for me."

He rubbed her thigh. "I'm sorry it was such a shitty day and a half."

"Yeah, me too," she sighed. "But Michaela is fine, and she felt supported by both of us, and that's all that matters."

"Is it, though?" Everett asked. "Maybe Michaela should know how badly her father treats her mother. Eventually, it will come out. People can't hide their true natures forever."

"You haven't met Gary," she said. "He's a politician, remember? He's an expert at hiding his horrible side."

"I don't think it's fair that Michaela blames you for everything," Everett said.

"It's not, but look, even if I tried to tell her that her dad isn't who she thinks he is, she wouldn't believe me. I've gone along with the pretense for too long now," Sierra said.

"You could try," Everett said.

"It isn't worth it," Sierra said. "It would cause tension between the three of us, and I won't hurt my relationship with Michaela because Gary's an asshole to me. I can handle his bullshit."

"All right," Everett said. "You know both of them best. It just worried me how exhausted and sad you looked tonight."

"Such a charmer," she said teasingly.

He just rolled his eyes and drank some water. She studied him briefly before saying, "So, do you and your ex get along?"

"We don't talk to each other much. When Taylor lived here, she split holidays and birthdays between us, and now that she's older, there isn't any reason for Wendy and I to talk."

"Why did you separate?" Sierra asked.

"She changed, and I didn't," he said.

His voice had no bitterness, just a hint of sorrow that made her take his hand. "I'm sorry."

"It's for the best," he said. "We were making each other miserable, and Taylor was starting to act out because of it."

"How old was she when you separated?" Sierra asked.

"Fifteen. After Wendy and I separated, she lived with me and spent every other weekend at her mom's place."

Surprise washed over Sierra, and Everett must have seen it on her face because he said, "Wendy's career came first, and being a mother came second. That was always obvious to Taylor, so she chose me when she needed to decide who to live with. Again, it was for the best. Both she and Wendy were happier not living together."

"Do they get along now?"

"Mostly," he said. "They're very different in personality, and Taylor has some resentment toward her mom. Apparently, they were doing therapy together before Taylor moved away, which helped. Although Wendy is pissed at her for staying another year in Japan, so there's some tension between them again."

"Has Wendy remarried?" Sierra asked.

"No, and I doubt she will. She has particular tastes in men." He paused. "She would like your ex-husband. Image is important to her as well."

"She sounds great," she said, mimicking Everett from earlier.

He laughed, but it sounded a bit forced, before he rubbed her leg. "Enough talking about our exes. Lie on your side, Sierra."

"Ooh, side sex, I love it," she said. She whipped off the towel and dropped it over the side of the bed before turning onto her side. Everett shut off the light and spooned her, his big hand cupping her breast.

She waited a few minutes, and when he didn't do anything, she rubbed her ass against his groin. He didn't respond, and she said, "Everett?"

"Yeah?"

"Isn't this the part where you stick your dick in me?"

He laughed and gave her breast a gentle squeeze. "You're exhausted, Sierra. Go to sleep."

"But you didn't get an orgasm," she said. "It isn't fair."

"You can give me one later," he said. "You need sleep."

"I don't need much sleep, so -" A giant yawn nearly cracked her jaw in two.

Everett pressed a kiss against the back of her shoulder. "Go to sleep, Sierra."

"Yes, Everett."

CHAPTER 15

Everett woke to the delightful sensation of Sierra kissing his chest. He palmed the back of her head, moaning when she sucked lightly on one flat nipple.

"Sierra?"

"Yeah?"

"What are you doing?"

She kissed her way down his stomach. "I'm about to suck your cock."

"It's four in the morning." He squinted at the alarm clock.

"It's later. You said we could have sex later." Her hot mouth slid down his dick, and any thought of stopping her vanished. He groaned and thrust into her mouth, his dick already impossibly hard and hot desire flooding his senses.

He grabbed her pillow and propped it under his head to give him a better view of her sucking his dick. "Fuck, sweetheart," he said, "you are so good at sucking cock."

She slid him out from between her lips and gave him a prim smile. "Thank you."

He wound her hair around his hand and tugged her back to his cock. "I didn't say to stop."

"Yes, Everett," she said, and another hot shiver of lust went through him.

She sucked hard on his dick, staring up at him obediently when he told her to. He loved how submissive she was with him, loved that he'd already gained her trust, and she wanted to please him.

He made her suck him until his balls tightened, and he could almost see how Sierra would look swallowing his seed as he pumped himself between her lips over and over. He pulled her off his dick in a hurry. One day he would come in her mouth and watch her swallow it, but this morning, he needed to fuck her.

"Do you want me on my hands and knees?" she asked sweetly.

He shook his head. "No, you're on top this time."

She climbed onto him eagerly, the brush of her pussy against his aching dick making him hiss out a breath. "Put me in you, Sierra."

She paused with her hand wrapped around his base. "You're good not to use a condom?"

"Yes." She'd emailed him her medical records, but he hadn't looked at them yet. He didn't need to. He trusted her.

"Thank fuck, because I want you bare inside of me," she said before she slid her pussy down over his dick.

"Fuuuuck," he groaned, his hands clamping onto her hips as her wet warmth encased his dick.

"Agreed," she panted before bouncing on him like he was a fucking trampoline.

He muttered a curse at the tight wet grip of her pussy and slapped her ass hard. "Sierra, stop."

She stopped moving but pouted at him. "I want to fuck you."

"Slowly," he said. "Fuck me slowly."

Her pout deepened, and he gave her ass another slap. She gasped and cried out, her little pussy squeezing him so tight he almost blew his load into her.

"Sierra," he gritted, his hands digging into her hips. "Stop squeezing."

She took a deep shuddering breath, and the iron grip of her pussy loosened enough that he was able to gain back some semblance of control. He cupped her tits, pulling and toying with her nipples until she was grinding against him with slow movements and moaning repeatedly.

"Please, Everett, can I fuck you?" she asked.

"Yes." He pinched her nipples hard. "Slowly, Sierra."

"Yes, Everett," she moaned before bracing her hands on his chest and rocking back and forth slowly.

He let her continue for a few minutes before squeezing her ass cheek. It was hot from his slaps, and he smiled with satisfaction. "Stop trying to get yourself off and fuck me properly."

"I want to come," she whined.

"You can come after I do," he said.

"That's not fair," she said.

He arched an eyebrow at her. "Keep complaining, and after I come, I'll spank you and deny you an orgasm."

She stilled on top of him, her look of horror making him grin. "You wouldn't."

"I would, Sierra. Do what I tell you, or you won't get to come."

She glared at him but stopped rocking against him and made slow thrusts instead. He relaxed against the bed, tucking his hands under his head and watching her pussy slide up and down his dick while he worked hard to keep his face calm. Sierra already liked to test boundaries with him. It would do him no favours if she knew how fucking close he was to coming already. Her tight little pussy felt incredible, and watching her perfect body ride him was a fantasy come to life.

He reached for her pussy, rubbing her swollen clit, and smiling at her soft cry of pleasure.

"You see, sweetheart? You do what I tell you, and you get rewarded."

Her thrusts lost their rhythm, and she rocked against his fingers again. Her fingers dug into his chest, and the look of hot need on her face shattered his control.

"Touch yourself," he demanded as he gripped her hips and thrust his cock deep into her pussy.

She rubbed frantically at her clit, her slender body shaking with every one of his thrusts. He pumped harder and faster, his release so fucking close, he could no longer hold back.

He shouted with pleasure as his orgasm rocketed through him, and he thrust harder. Sierra made a shrill cry, and her pussy gripped him tight, pulsing around him as she came.

"Fuck!" He flipped her onto her back, pounding hard into her as the last of his orgasm flooded through his body. She took every thrust, wrapping her legs around his waist even as they shook from her climax.

He rolled off before he collapsed on her, his body twitching wildly. She curled up into him, and he pressed a kiss against her mouth. "Holy fuck, Sierra."

"Agreed," she said, nestling in against him. She was already starting to fall asleep, and he cupped her ass, pulling her in tight against him before closing his eyes.

"WHY DOES MY HOUSE SMELL SO DELICIOUS?" SIERRA wandered into the kitchen. She wore a t-shirt and leggings and had grout smeared across the front of her shirt.

Everett stirred the pasta sauce before grinning at her. "That's a lot of grout on your shirt."

"I know, right? I had an unfortunate grouting accident while working on the backsplash," Sierra said. "Are you cooking?"

"I am," he said.

She made a soft squeak of excitement. "Are you doing something nice for me because of the amazing orgasm I gave you this morning?"

He laughed again. "The orgasm was fantastic, but I'm cooking because I enjoy it."

He stirred the sauce again as Sierra plopped her butt onto one of the kitchen stools. He'd meant to go home to shower and change before starting work on the basement, but after their early morning sex, he and Sierra had slept in until almost eight. He'd had a quick shower in her guest bathroom and went straight to work in the basement.

At noon, Sierra came downstairs with a sandwich and fruit for him. She had plans to meet a friend for lunch, so she'd given him a quick kiss and left.

He heard her return around two, but she hadn't come downstairs, and he'd been too busy to check in with her. When he finished and came upstairs to the main floor around five, she was upstairs working on the bathroom.

He'd told himself to leave. He'd been at Sierra's house nonstop since yesterday morning, and if he stayed tonight, too, she would get the wrong idea.

As much as he enjoyed his time with her, he couldn't date her. Not when it would end the same way it ended with Wendy. Sierra enjoyed fucking him. Hell, she might even think it would be fun to date him for a while, but eventually, she'd get tired of their differences, and they'd be finished. She'd walk away with nothing but good memories while he was left with a bruised and bleeding heart.

He already had feelings for her that would cause him nothing but heartache, which was why he should have left. Instead, he'd gone into her kitchen and started cooking her fucking dinner.

"You know," Sierra said, "I've never dated someone who liked to cook."

Fuck.

He *really* should have left earlier.

He turned to face her, and at the look on his face, Sierra said, "Oh God, I just screwed up, didn't I?"

"No," he said.

"I did. I made an assumption about the dating thing, and now I look like an asshole."

"You don't," he said. "I'm the asshole for not being clear about what I was looking for before we started sleeping together. Life is busy right now, and I'd prefer something casual."

Embarrassment coating her face, Sierra nodded. "Sure, I get it."

Feeling stupid, he stirred the pasta sauce again as a thick silence filled the kitchen. After a few seconds, he said, "If you're looking for exclusivity and something more than casual, I get it and -"

"Casual's fine," Sierra said. Her voice sounded weird, and he turned to face her again.

"Is it?" he asked.

She nodded and smiled at him, although it looked a little off to him. "Yes. I'm good with casual."

"It's okay if it isn't," he said. "You don't have to say it is because you know that's what I want to hear."

Her laugh was a bit more natural. "Sorry, but have you met me? Saying something to make a person happy isn't exactly my style."

She slid off the stool. "I'll change my shirt and be back to set the table. Be right back."

"Sierra," he said.

She paused in the doorway and gave him a bright smile. "Yes?"

"It has nothing to do with you," he lied. "It's just where I am in my life right now."

"I get it," she said, "and casual is okily-dokily with me."

She left the kitchen, and his stomach bubbling and twisting like the pasta in the pot, Everett turned the heat down on the sauce.

That had gone fucking awful.

Because you lied to her. You like Sierra, and you lied to her about it. You made her feel like she was only worth a casual relationship. You are such an asshole.

Yeah, he really was. But he couldn't have more with Sierra, not when it would break his heart.

CHAPTER 16

"You're telling me that the words 'okily dokily' actually came out of your mouth," Hazel said.

"Yes," Sierra groaned before leaning over and whacking her forehead on the steering wheel.

"What's that sound?" Indie asked.

Sierra had called Hazel on her cell and conferenced Indie in after Hazel declared she needed backup to handle the situation.

"It's me trying to smack some sense back into myself," Sierra said.

The sound of dogs barking drowned out whatever Indie said in reply. After a few seconds, the sound dimmed, and Indie said, "Sorry. I'm in my office now with the door shut. Listen, I've only got five minutes before my next appointment, so we need to solve this fast."

"There isn't anything to solve," Sierra said.

"Other than you using the phrase 'okily dokily'," Hazel said.

"Focus, Hazel," Sierra said.

"Sorry," Hazel said. "And I'm sorry that Everett is being a dickhead."

"He isn't," Sierra said. "I'm glad he was honest with me about what he wanted."

"But you weren't honest with him," Indie said gently.

"How could I be?" Sierra sighed. "If I'd told him that I wanted more than casual, that would have been it for us, and I can't lose the sex, Indie. My God, the sex is amazing. The man can practically spank me into an orgasm."

"Oh my God," Indie said.

Hazel laughed. "On a scale of pink to firehouse red, what colour is your face right now, Indie?"

"It's like the red light district in my office," Indie said.

Despite her misery, Sierra couldn't help but laugh. "I love you, Indie."

"I love you too, honey, and I'm so sorry it's not working out how you want with Everett."

"Thanks," Sierra said. "I mean, it could be worse, right? He could have just cut me off completely from the best sex of my life when I said that stupid thing about dating."

"In your defense, based on what you just shared with us, it sounds like you were dating. He's helping you with your renovations in his free time, running you a bath, making you dinner... those aren't things a guy looking for casual does. He's sending major mixed messages."

"He *was*," Sierra said. "He's definitely not now."

"What do you mean?" Hazel asked.

Sierra sighed. "It's clear this is about sex and nothing else now. I knew he wouldn't stick around after he finished working on the basement yesterday, so I made sure I was in the shower when he usually finishes work for the day. I didn't want to deal with the awkwardness of him leaving when he usually stays for dinner. But he was in the bedroom waiting for me when I finished showering."

"What happened?"

"He fucked the bejeezus out of me and then went home," Sierra said.

"Oh," Indie said.

"What was today like?" Hazel asked.

"I didn't see him," Sierra said. "I didn't bring him lunch because I didn't want him to think I wanted more from him, and I spent all day upstairs working on the bathroom. At three, I got a text from him saying he was leaving early for a meeting, and he left without saying goodbye."

"Sorry, honey," Hazel said.

"It's fine," Sierra said. "I just wish it wasn't so awkward between us now. I'm okay with casual, but -"

"Are you?" Indie asked. "Because it sounds like you really like this guy."

Sierra muttered a curse. "I do. I really do. But I need to be okay with casual because that's all he wants."

"Since when did you do something just because a guy wanted you to?" Hazel asked.

"Since I met Everett Caine," Sierra said. "Which pisses me off because I shouldn't be doing that, but it's like he has me under some kind of dick spell."

Hazel and Indie started laughing, and Sierra leaned her head against the headrest. "Why am I being like this?"

"Because you're falling in love with him," Indie said.

"Cork it, Indiana," Sierra said. "I'm not in love with a guy who wants nothing but sex from me."

"Not yet, but you will be soon, so maybe you should end this," Indie said. "I don't mean to be a total bummer, but ending it'll be much harder once you're well and truly in love with him."

"She's right," Hazel said. "I know this isn't what you want to hear, honey, but you're only setting yourself up for heartache."

"I know," Sierra said. "I need to end it, but even the thought of not seeing him makes me get all weird and sad inside. God, why does life have to be so complicated? I finally found a funny and sweet guy who can drywall the hell out of my house and does it for me in bed, but he only wants me for sex. What kind of fucking luck is that?"

"The worst luck," Indie said. "Shit. I have to go to my appointment. I'm sorry I had to cancel our weekly dinner tonight, ladies."

"It's fine," Hazel said. "I had to cancel too, remember?"

"Okay, I really gotta go. Love you both!" Indie ended the call.

"Honey, if you don't want to be alone tonight, I can cancel with Spencer and Preston," Hazel said.

"No, you can't," Sierra said. "It's their tux fittings, and I know how much it means to you that Spencer wants you there for it. I'm fine, babe, I promise."

"What are you doing tonight?"

"I'm at the Grill and Pour Tavern. I'm going to have a beer, eat my weight in chicken tenders and fries, and then go home," Sierra said.

"Okay. Well, if you change your mind, text me. I'll join you," Hazel said.

"It's all good. Tell Spence and Preston I said hi, and I'll text you tomorrow." Sierra ended the call, shut off the car, and headed into the restaurant. Her phone buzzed as she opened the front door, and she snagged it from her pocket, smiling a little when she saw Michaela's text.

Her gaze on her phone, she grunted when she ran into

something warm and solid. She backed away and said, "I'm so sorry, I wasn't paying... Everett?"

"Sierra, hi," Everett said.

"Hi. What are you doing here?" she asked and then winced inwardly. "Sorry, that isn't any of my business."

"I was supposed to be meeting a client for dinner and drinks, but they just bailed on me," Everett said.

He wore a long-sleeved burgundy shirt with a pair of casual pants, and he'd trimmed his beard. He smelled amazing and looked damn sexy, and a sliver of jealousy went through her. Was his client a woman?

"I'm sorry she bailed on you," Sierra said.

Christ, could she be any more obvious?

"He," Everett said, "and it's not the first time. This was his last chance, and the next time he texts, I'll stop wasting my time and let him know he can find someone else."

She tried to think of anything else to say to keep him with her for a bit longer. It'd only been twenty-four hours since she'd seen him last, but she missed him.

"So, are you meeting friends here?" Everett asked.

She shook her head. "No, they had to cancel, so I'm soloing dinner tonight."

Oh God, she sounded like such a loser.

"You could join me. If you want," she said. "Totally casual, no expectations for anything more."

He cleared his throat, and she forced a smile on her face. "Never mind. That was inappropriate of me to suggest, and I apologize. Have a great night. I'll see you tomorrow."

God, she hated that she could ask him to fuck her and know she'd get a yes, but a simple dinner invite made him run for the hills.

He caught her arm. "Sierra, wait. I'd like to have dinner with you."

"It's okay," she said. "I don't need a pity dinner."

He gave her an irritated look. "We're friends too, Sierra. This isn't a pity dinner. This is me accepting a dinner invite from a friend."

"All right," she said, "don't get your panties in a bunch over it. God."

He stepped closer and leaned in so only she could hear him. "Keep talking that way, and I'll spank you so hard when we get home that you won't be able to sit for a week."

"Promises, promises," she said, her voice embarrassingly breathy.

He grinned at her before straightening. "Let's find a table."

"OH MY GOD," SIERRA LAUGHED. "TEENAGE GIRLS ARE THE worst."

"Right?" Everett popped a fry into his mouth. "Taylor was grounded for a month after that little stunt."

Sierra dipped her chicken tender into the plum sauce. "All things considered, Michaela was a pretty easy teenager, but her attitude was a killer. I used to call my mom daily to whine, and she'd laugh and remind me that I was the same way as a teenager. There was zero sympathy from her."

Everett grinned. "Secretly, I think grandparents love it when their grandchildren are little monsters. It's karma."

Sierra laughed again. "So, you won't be sympathetic to Taylor when she calls to complain about her kids, is what you're saying."

"Exactly," Everett said, his grin widening. "Plus, I'll be the grandpa that feeds them a bunch of sugar and then sends them home."

"Diabolical," Sierra said. "Does Taylor want kids?"

"She does," Everett said. "She's not so sure she wants a husband, so she's considering artificial insemination and adoption options. What about Michaela?"

"She's not sure yet. She's pansexual and currently dating a trans guy, but I don't think it's to the point where they're discussing marriage or kids. She's introduced David to Gary and me, and we both like him, but I get the impression that he might be a little more serious about the relationship than Michaela is." Sierra sipped at her beer.

Everett ate another fry. "It's good that -"

"Sierra?"

The familiar voice sent dismay rocketing through Sierra. She tensed and glanced at the man who'd stopped at their booth. He was short with thick brown hair, an olive-coloured complexion, and dark brown eyes. His bushy eyebrows raised a notch as he stared at her and then at Everett.

Fuck. It would be just her luck to run into Richard fucking Dalton. He was a fellow judge and a misogynistic asshole who didn't believe women should be judges, and he had a God complex.

Even worse, he was friends with Gary. At least, he believed he was. Gary only used Richard for his connections, but Richard was too arrogant to see it.

As he eyed Everett up and down, Sierra knew that he would immediately text Gary about what he'd seen tonight, like the fucking little rat he was. And like always, Gary would be on her fucking ass about who she was dating, if it was serious, had Michaela met him. On one memorial occasion, Gary had tracked down some poor guy she was only casually fucking and grilled him about Sierra for nearly ten minutes before the guy could escape.

Gary was just as much a control freak as she was, and it

didn't seem to matter that they'd been divorced for six years. He still thought he could tell Sierra what she could or couldn't do.

With a polite smile, she said, "How are you, Richard?"

"Can't complain." He eyed her chicken tenders and fries. "It's always nice to see a woman eat without worrying about her weight."

Sierra could barely stop from rolling her eyes. Richard believing she gave one fuck what he thought of her looks was so goddamn typical of him she couldn't even muster the strength to be annoyed.

"Richard Dalton. I work at the courthouse with Sierra." Richard held his hand out to Everett.

Everett shook it and, with a bland smile, said, "Nice to meet you. Are you Sierra's court clerk?"

Sierra turned her laugh into a cough as Richard's face reddened. "Hardly. I'm a judge. I've been a judge for longer than Sierra has."

"Good for you." Everett's voice was thick with conde-scension.

Richard's nostrils flared. "How long have you and Sierra been dating?"

Shit. She needed to shut this down quickly.

"We're not dating," she said. "Everett is my drywaller."

"You're a drywaller," Richard said to Everett. Sierra could almost see the disdain in Richard's eyes. He was as big a snob as her ex-husband.

She ignored her urge to defend Everett. One, there was nothing to defend, and two, if she showed any type of strong reaction to or about Everett, Richard wouldn't hesitate to tell Gary.

"That's right," Everett said. His voice was steady and calm, but Sierra could see red creeping up his neck.

"Do you always have an intimate dinner with your drywaller?" Richard asked Sierra.

This time, she did roll her eyes. "We're discussing the work he's doing on my house, and I'd hardly say that chicken tenders and beers at a fucking pub is intimate, Richard. Everett is a contractor I've hired and nothing more."

She glanced at Everett, surprised by the hurt on his face. It disappeared quickly, leaving her uncertain if it had ever really been there. Everett gave her a polite, almost bored smile before taking a sip of beer and dismissing Richard entirely.

Sierra smiled frostily at Richard. "Enjoy your evening, Richard."

"You as well." With one final glance at Everett, he walked away.

Sierra waited until Richard was out of earshot before saying, "Sorry about that. He's -"

"It's fine." Everett's neck was still red, and he looked pissed. "You don't have to explain."

"Everett, are you okay?" she asked.

"Yes." He dug his wallet out of his pocket. "But I have to get going."

"Wait, what?" She watched in disbelief as he tossed some bills on the table.

"This should cover my cost for dinner," he said.

"Everett, wait," she said as he slid out of the booth. "I thought…"

He raised an impatient eyebrow at her. "What?"

"I thought you would come back to my house tonight," she said.

"I can't, but I'll see you tomorrow." He gave her a grim, tension-filled smile and left.

She sat back in the booth, staring at the money Everett

had left on the table. Their server arrived, and she stared blankly at him when he said, "Would you like another beer?"

Her brain whirling, she shook her head. "No, thanks. Just the bill, please."

He nodded and left, returning a few minutes later with the bill. She paid, left Everett's money on the table as a tip, and hurried out of the restaurant. She scanned the parking lot, looking for Everett's truck, even though she knew he'd already be gone.

Her confusion was starting to fade, leaving annoyance to take its place. She had no idea what the fuck Everett's problem was, but it was super shitty of him to just walk away without any explanation. She stalked toward her car and slid behind the wheel, jabbing her finger angrily against the start button. Everett was treating her like shit, and she didn't care how much she liked him. She didn't date men who -

You're not dating.

Her annoyance blinked out. They weren't dating. It didn't matter that tonight's dinner had felt like a date. It wasn't. Everett had been clear about what he wanted from her, and it wasn't a relationship. He owed her no explanations for his behaviour tonight, and she had no right to be angry with him.

Her phone rang, and she studied the unfamiliar number before pressing the answer button. "Sierra Lewis speaking."

"Hi, Sierra. This is Mac, Val Jensen's friend. We met at Indie and Val's place last week."

"Hi, Mac. How are you?"

"Good, thank you. Indie gave me your number. Is this a bad time for you?"

"I'm just about to drive home," she said as she leaned her head against the headrest and closed her eyes.

"I won't keep you for long then. I wondered if you'd like to have dinner with me on Friday," Mac said.

Sierra lifted her head, her eyes popping open. "Dinner? With you?"

He laughed. "Dinner. With me."

She stared out the windshield. The restaurant's neon sign gave everything it touched an eerie blue glow. Mac was asking her out on a date.

Everett will be pissed if you go out with Mac.

No, he wouldn't. He didn't expect exclusivity. He said that himself. For all she knew, he could have a dozen other women on the side. He was certainly hot enough to be fucking multiple women.

"Sierra? Are you still there?" Mac asked. "Shit. Did I lose the connection?"

"No, I'm here. Sorry," she said. "I was… um… yes, I'll have dinner with you on Friday."

"Great," Mac said. "Do you like sushi? There's a great sushi place on the west side of town called Sushi of the Sea. Don't let the cheesy name fool you. It's amazing."

"I like sushi," she said. "I could meet you there Friday around seven?"

"Perfect," Mac said. "I'll see you then."

"See you then," she echoed and ended the call.

She sat in her car, anxiety curling at her edges and fighting the urge to call Mac back and cancel. She felt weirdly guilty about going out with him, which pissed her off. She and Everett weren't dating, and why should she just sit around having sex with him and not meeting anyone else? She didn't want to be alone for the rest of her life, and Mac seemed like a good guy. She'd enjoyed his company at the barbecue. She'd go out with him Friday night and not think of stupid Everett Caine even once.

What happens if Everett wants to fuck on Friday night? Then what?

She'd tell him she had other plans. Her life didn't revolve around Everett.

You're telling me if Everett didn't give you that look, didn't ask you in that goddamn sexy voice of his if you wanted to go upstairs and be spanked, you wouldn't bail on Mac without a second's hesitation?

She smacked the steering wheel. Fuck! She didn't want to admit it, didn't want to be that type of person, but there was a big possibility that she would do just that. Resisting Everett was as impossible as breathing underwater.

She grabbed her phone and sent off a quick text to Michaela. She would drive up to see Michaela again early tomorrow morning. She'd grab a hotel close to the university, take a little mini vacation and spend some time with her kid without Gary butting in. She'd drive back Friday night in time for her date with Mac and go straight to the restaurant.

She wouldn't be tempted by Everett Caine, and everything would be fine.

Everything would be just fine.

CHAPTER 17

"It was good to see you, Everett. We need to do this more often." Rob held out his hand, and Everett shook it.

"Agreed. Tell Roxie I said hi, and let me know if you get that roofing job."

"Will do. Thanks again for recommending me." Rob stood up from the table, and Everett stood as well.

"I need to use the restroom before I head out," Everett said.

"Talk to you soon, buddy." Rob headed toward the exit as Everett walked toward the restrooms. He hadn't seen Rob in a while, and he'd tried hard to concentrate on his friend, but he wondered if his distraction was as noticeable to Rob as it was to him.

Distraction? That's a mild word for your obsession with Sierra.

He used the restroom and washed his hands, staring at himself in the mirror over the sink. He looked normal, but his insides were a sudsy mess and had been since he woke up to a text yesterday morning from Sierra.

It was short and simple. She was going out of town, and

she'd see him on Monday morning. He could help himself to anything in the fridge and text her if there were any problems with the basement.

He reached for his phone and reread the text for about the thousandth time since Thursday morning. It was a perfectly fine, perfectly *cordial* text. The polite text a person would send to the contractor working on their home, not to the man who'd seen her naked, had his tongue in her pussy, and spanked her ass until it glowed.

He muttered a curse and shoved his phone into his pocket. He'd been pissed on Wednesday night when he left her in the restaurant. He'd handled the situation like a fucking pouting baby, and over the last couple of days, he'd regretted it more and more.

Sierra treating him like he meant nothing to her in front of her coworker shouldn't have been a shock, but it was. He knew who she was and that she wouldn't want her peers to know she was with someone like Everett, but seeing it for himself had been a brutal blow.

You're the one who said casual, who said no relationship, remember? She was just following the rules.

Maybe, but there'd been real anxiety in her face and voice when she'd seen her coworker. Even just the idea that he might think Sierra was dating Everett had been enough to upset her.

So, it proves you made the right decision to keep it casual. Good for you.

Yeah, good for fucking him.

He left the bathroom and headed toward the exit. The smart thing to do would be to stop fucking Sierra. Every time he slept with her, every time he *kissed* her, he lost a little more of his heart to her. If he kept this up, his heart would be nothing but a tattered...

He slowed to a stop, staring in disbelief at the couple sitting at the table to his left. The man was in a wheelchair and grinned at the woman sitting across from him, a platter piled high with sushi on the table between them.

The woman was Sierra.

His brain screaming at him to keep walking toward the exit, Everett headed toward them like his body was on autopilot. He stopped in front of their table as the man said, "We definitely ordered too much sushi. I hope you're prepared to…"

He trailed off, staring up at Everett with a puzzled look on his face. "Hey, can we help you?"

Sierra glanced up, her gaze going wide. She wore a dark blue dress that clung to her perfect body, and her hair and makeup were carefully done. He stared at her red painted lips and shoved his jealousy deep. Maybe they were just friends.

"Everett? Um, hi," she said.

"Hello, Sierra. I thought you were out of town," Everett said.

"I just got back tonight," she said.

There was an awkward silence that he felt in every one of his bones.

"This is Everett. He's my contractor. Everett, this is Mac. He's my, uh…" Sierra hesitated.

The man held out his hand and said, "Date. Nice to meet you, Everett."

Everett shook his hand, barely able to stop his caveman urge to tell Mac not to even think of fucking Sierra. "Nice to meet you."

He turned back to Sierra, smiling stiffly at her. "Enjoy your evening, Sierra."

"Thanks, you as well," she said.

He walked away, shoving his hands into his pockets to keep Sierra from seeing how they twisted into fists.

SIERRA PARKED IN HER DRIVEWAY AND SHUT OFF THE CAR before pressing the palms of her hands against her eyes.

"Am I cursed?" she asked the empty car. "Is that what this is? Did I piss off some deity, and that's why I keep running into Everett fucking Caine everywhere I go?"

She sighed deeply. The rest of her date with Mac had gone fine. Well, if you call hiding her urge to vomit, fine. Everett stumbling onto her date with Mac had rattled her badly.

Mac had escorted her to her car after dinner and had been polite and said all the right things, but she knew he wouldn't call her again. Why would he? The date had been a fucking disaster the minute Everett had shown up.

It wasn't going well before that, and you know it. Maybe not in a way that Mac noticed, but even if Everett hadn't shown up, you wouldn't be going out with Mac again. Admit it.

"Fuck!" she shouted and smacked her hands against the steering wheel.

Mac was a great guy and funny as hell, but she'd felt nothing during her date with him. Even before seeing Everett, she couldn't stop thinking about him, just like she'd done the last two days. She'd been so distracted by thoughts of Everett that even Michaela had noticed.

She grabbed her purse and climbed out of the car, slamming the door and locking it before walking toward the house. She climbed the stairs and reached to punch the key code in. Her fingers paused over the keypad, and her heart thudding, she turned her head to the right.

Everett sat on her porch in one of the wicker chairs, his face nearly hidden in shadows. She stared silently at him for almost a minute before she punched the key code in with trembling fingers. She stepped inside the house and walked to the kitchen, leaving the door wide open. She grabbed a bottle of water from the fridge and opened it, taking a long swallow to ease her suddenly dry throat.

Her heart pounding in her ears, she faced the window, gripping the sink as the door shut, and she heard Everett's footsteps in the kitchen. She released her breath in a shuddering sigh when his arm slid around her body. He cupped her breast, squeezing roughly as he swept aside her hair and kissed the side of her throat.

She moaned when he pinched her nipple and then nipped her throat hard enough to leave a mark. His big hand pressed against her upper back, and she leaned over the counter, her fingers digging into the cold porcelain as Everett gripped the hem of her dress and tugged it to her waist.

She wore a thong under it, and she heard his sharp inhale of breath just before his warm hand caressed her ass cheeks. She moaned and arched, spreading her legs willingly when Everett nudged at them with his knee.

He kept one hand on her back while the other stroked and kneaded her ass. His fingers dipped between her legs and brushed lightly against her soaked panties.

He retreated almost immediately, and she whined in disappointment. "Everett, touch -"

The sound of his hand spanking her bare ass cheek was shockingly loud in the quiet kitchen. She squealed in surprise and pain, her body jerking against the sink. He pressed harder on her back, pinning her against the counter and the sink before spanking her hard and fast.

It hurt like hell, but there was pleasure in the pain, and she stopped fighting him, accepting her punishment as he spanked her with a slow and deliberate rhythm.

He stopped spanking her and threaded his hand through her hair, pulling her into a standing position. He unzipped her dress and yanked it over her head, tossing it onto the table before he unhooked her bra and pulled it from her body.

He pressed his body against hers, and she ground her throbbing ass against his erection. He made a sound of disapproval and pulled her hair hard, yanking her head back and giving her another slap on the ass.

She melted against him, trembling lightly as he cupped her breasts with his free hand. He pulled and tugged on her nipples, pinching them until she cried out.

He used her hair to turn her face toward his. He kissed her hard, forcing her mouth open to thrust his tongue deep inside. She was so turned on she could barely breathe, and she wanted to beg him to fuck her. Instead, she submitted to his rough touch and his need to dominate her.

He released her mouth and studied her in the dim light from the window. "Did you fuck him, Sierra?"

"No," she said.

She assumed that would make him happy, maybe even convince him to fuck her, so when he bent her over the sink again and spanked her ass even harder, she cried out in surprise. She wiggled against him and tried to protect her burning ass with her hands. He pushed them away and spanked her repeatedly.

Tears leaked down her face, her nipples rock hard, and her pussy throbbing and aching to be filled, she gripped the counter and absorbed each of his spanks in silent submission.

When he pulled her straight again, he turned her head toward him and gently wiped away the tears from her cheeks.

"Did you want to fuck him, Sierra?"

"No," she said. "No, I only want to fuck you, Everett."

His look of approval made her so damn hot. Was it possible for someone to spontaneously combust from lust?

"Everett," she begged, "please fuck me."

He squeezed her breasts, toying with her nipples as he pressed a gentle kiss against her cheek. "Do you think you deserve to be fucked?"

"Yes," she said. "I'm being good for you, Everett."

"Hmm," he said, sliding his hand down her stomach and into her panties. He cupped her pussy, his fingers gliding through the slick wetness. "You're very wet, sweetheart. You're wet because of the spanking, aren't you?"

"Yes," she said.

He chuckled, his fingers grazing against her swollen clit. "Maybe your punishment should be a spanking and no fucking."

"No!" Her cry sounded half-hysterical. If Everett didn't fuck her, she'd lose her goddamn mind. "Everett, you have to fuck me. Please."

He gave her clit a sharp pinch that hurt but also nearly made her come all over his hand. "I don't have to do anything, sweetheart."

"Please," she begged, rubbing her throbbing ass against his cock. "Everett, please."

He pulled her away from the counter, spinning her around and pushing her up against the table with rough, hard movements. He pushed her down over the table, forcing her upper body flat against it. He fisted her hair, turning her head so she could see him. "Don't you fucking move, Sierra."

"I won't," she moaned.

He trailed his hand down her back and hooked his fingers into her thong. He pulled it down her legs and off her feet, leaving her just in her heels. He pushed at her knee. "Spread your legs for me."

She spread them, and he slapped her ass, making her gasp and jerk. "I know you can spread them wider than that, Sierra."

She spread her legs until she felt the burn in her thigh muscles. Everett gripped her ass cheeks, spreading them apart and tracing his finger across her anus.

"I'm going to fuck this beautiful ass this weekend."

Her stomach clenched with pleasure, and fresh liquid dripped from her pussy. Everett ran his fingers over her pussy and made a low chuckle. "Someone likes that idea. Is that what you want, Sierra? Me buried balls deep in this absolutely fucking perfect ass?"

He slapped her ass. "Answer me."

"Yes," she said. "I want you to fuck my ass, Everett."

"Good," he said.

He took off his shirt and unbuttoned and unzipped his jeans. She turned her head and watched as he pulled his cock free and rubbed it slowly. She licked her lips when a bead of precum slicked the head. Everett laughed again. "Maybe I should put you on your knees and fuck your mouth instead of your tight pussy."

She swallowed hard. "Whatever you want, Everett."

Another look of approval that made her entire body scream for him. "Good answer, sweetheart. Close your eyes."

She rested her hot cheek against the cool wood of the table and closed her eyes. She could barely hear over her pounding heart, and she hoped desperately that Everett would fuck her. If he didn't, she -

She screamed and reared up at the first touch of Everett's

tongue against her pussy. He growled at her and slapped her ass hard. "Don't fucking move, I said."

She grabbed the other side of the table, holding it tightly as Everett gripped her thighs and leaned in to lick her pussy. Glassy-eyed and shivering wildly, she moaned, "Oh, Everett, please, honey. Please."

He ignored her, using his tongue to clean the cream from her lips and investigate her hole as she moaned, begged, and squirmed against the table. When his tongue finally slicked across her throbbing clit, she squeezed the table and shouted his name.

He held her down and licked her clit with flat broad strokes before sucking it into his mouth. She shrieked until her voice cracked and came all over Everett's face, her orgasm roaring through her like an avalanche.

Hot lightning crashed through her, flooding every nerve ending and making her body buck. Everett shoved his cock into her pussy, and she cried out when he fucked her so hard her feet left the floor. He muttered a curse and grabbed her hips, holding her in a tight grip as he fucked her with rough, deep strokes.

She clung to the table, her body taking every one of his strokes as Everett made a nearly feral sound of pleasure and slapped her ass. She cried out, squeezing her pussy around his cock in a tight grip.

"Fuck!" Everett shouted before pumping in and out of her furiously. The table scraped across the floor, and the water glass she'd left on the table fell off the edge and shattered on the floor.

Everett shouted her name, his fingers digging into her hips, and hot wetness flooded her pussy. She squeezed around him, her body shuddering as Everett moaned and made a few final thrusts before his body slowed.

He leaned over her, his body pressed against hers and his hot breath against her shoulder. She could feel the rapid beat of his heart against her back, and when she stirred underneath him, he straightened and pulled out of her.

He helped her straighten without speaking and smiled at her as he brushed her hair from her sweaty cheeks. He rubbed her ass, satisfaction crossing his face when she hissed out a breath.

He pressed a kiss against her mouth, and she said, "Will you stay the night with me, Everett?"

"Yes," he said.

She tugged him toward the door, anxious to get him upstairs.

"The glass is broken," he said, pointing to the gleam of shattered glass on the floor.

"I'll clean it up in the morning," she said. "Come have a shower with me."

He squeezed her hand. "Whatever you want, Sierra."

CHAPTER 18

Sierra poured two cups of coffee and added milk to one and sugar to the other. She winced when she returned the milk to the fridge and rubbed at her arms and then her thighs. Her entire body ached. Who knew that a marathon day of sex would make her body hurt more than house renovations?

She sipped at her coffee, welcoming the jolt of caffeine. She and Everett had spent Saturday in bed, alternating between sex and napping with occasional breaks for eating and showering. She didn't think she'd ever spent an entire day fucking someone, not even in her twenties. Was it any wonder she felt like she'd been run over by a truck?

Still, if Everett wanted to fuck her all day today, she wouldn't say no. The mind-rattling orgasms were worth a little body ache. Although, she touched her ass gingerly, she'd have to take a pass on the spankings today. Which was unfortunate because they made her orgasms even better, but she could barely sit at this point.

She carried the coffee mugs out to the backyard. It was a gorgeous and quiet Sunday morning in her neighbourhood, and she handed one of the mugs to Everett, who sat at the patio table in just his jeans. Despite the unseasonably warm spring, she hadn't put out her cushioned seating yet, and she eyed the hard metal chairs with trepidation.

Everett patted his lap. "Sit here, sweetheart."

She sank onto his lap, hissing out a breath at the pressure on her ass. He rubbed her hip, a genuine look of regret on his face. "Sorry, Sierra. I shouldn't have spanked you as much as I did yesterday."

"I liked it a lot," she said, "so no need to apologize. That being said, no spankings today. My poor ass needs a break."

He pressed a kiss against her upper chest. "No spankings today."

They sipped at their coffees in mutual silence for a few minutes. She could get used to this, Sierra decided. Since her divorce, she'd loved living alone, but waking up to Everett in her bed this morning had brought a feeling of happiness she hadn't felt in a very long time.

It wasn't just the sex either. Everett was smart, funny, and kind. His laid-back attitude was the perfect contrast to her control issues, and he ran his own business and had a fantastic relationship with his kid. How he was still single, she had no fucking idea.

Because he's not looking for a relationship, remember? While you're busy falling in love with him, he's looking at you as nothing more than a casual fling. Don't let love blind you, Sierra.

Yeah, well, for someone who only wanted casual, he seemed to get pretty riled up over her date with Mac.

He's a Scorpio. They're the jealous, possessive type. Don't read anything more into it, or you'll set yourself up for a world of hurt.

"Hey, you good?" Everett rubbed her thigh. "You have a look on your face."

"It's my 'can I convince Everett to spend today with me as well,' look," she said.

He laughed and squeezed her leg. "No convincing required. Although, as much as it shames me to say this, I can't do another marathon day of fucking. I do one more hip thrust, and my back will lock up on me, and you'll have to drag my body to a chiropractor. You'd find that sexy, though, right?"

She laughed. "So damn sexy, Everett."

He grinned at her. "This is what happens when you fuck an old guy. We require more maintenance and upkeep."

"You're not old," she said. "And besides, I'm sore as well. I just hide it better because women are tougher than men."

"Is that right?" He arched an eyebrow at her before squeezing her thigh again. "So, you could take another spanking today. Is that what you're saying?"

"Fuck, no," she said. "But I could spank you even with these aching muscles."

"What a sweet offer," he said, "but I'm always the spanker, never the spankee."

"Nothing wrong with trying something different," she said teasingly. "You never know - it could be a secret kink for you."

He cupped the back of her neck and tugged her mouth down to his. "In a few days, when your ass is healed, sweet Sierra, expect to be put over my knee and spanked for your impertinence today."

Warmth unfurled in her belly, and she brushed her mouth repeatedly against his. He parted his lips and deepened the kiss. Despite her soreness, the familiar ache of lust washed over Sierra. Fuck, she wanted this man.

"You know," she said as Everett's big hand cupped her breast, "we could have sex again without you having to do any potential back destroying hip thrusts. Riding you like a pony is one of my new favourite things."

"Is that right?" He rubbed his thumb over her hardening nipple before sucking on her bottom lip.

She moaned softly, running her fingers across his warm chest. "Yes, in fact -"

"Mom?"

Michaela's voice had her scrambling from Everett's lap like he was on fire. Hot coffee slopped out of her cup, burning her hand. She cursed and set the mug on the table.

She stared in shock at her kid, who stood in the doorway leading out to the patio. "Michaela? What are you doing here?"

"I was worried about you," Michaela said. "You were acting so weird on Thursday and Friday, I figured I'd drive down today and do a vibe check."

"I'm fine," Sierra said.

Michaela grinned at her and Everett. "Obviously. Sorry, I didn't mean to interrupt your... coffee?"

Sierra wanted to barf. She'd had no intention of ever introducing Everett and Michaela. Not when all Everett wanted was something casual, and not when she knew Michaela would immediately tell Gary about Everett.

Everett stood, and Michaela eyed him up and down with her usual brashness before holding out her hand. "Hey, I'm Michaela."

"Everett." He shook her hand, and Sierra's urge to vomit worsened when Michaela's eyes widened.

"Shit. You're the contractor, right?" She turned to Sierra,

a look of delight on her face. "You're banging your contractor? That's lit."

"Michaela," Sierra said. "Stop."

"What? I'm not a kid, Mom. It's not like I don't know you have sex."

Her face flaming, Sierra took Michaela's arm and steered her inside. Everett followed them and disappeared out of the kitchen as Sierra tried not to let her desperation show on her face.

She didn't want Michaela to say anything to Gary, but asking her not to would raise too many questions. They were supposed to be one big happy family, and asking Michaela to keep a secret from her father would pop that happy family bubble like a hot poker.

Oblivious to Sierra's distress, Michaela grinned at her. "Nice work, Mom. He's a snack for an old guy."

"Michaela, I…"

Everett appeared in the kitchen doorway. He had thrown on his shirt and wore his boots. "I'm going to go, Sierra."

"No, don't," Michaela said. "You should, like, hang out with us. Do you like the farmers market? I was gonna ask Mom if she wanted to go to the farmers market. You should come with us. Right, Mom?"

Sierra wanted to groan in frustration. Explaining to her kid that Everett wasn't interested in her for anything more than sex was not on her fucking to-do list today.

Everett hadn't said anything, and Sierra could see Michaela winding up to be her 'lovable but sometimes pushy' self.

She spoke quickly before Michaela could say anything else. "Everett needs to get going, honey. Right, Everett?"

Hurt splashed across Everett's face, which confused the fuck out of Sierra, but she had no time to deal with it. Not when she had to figure out how to handle the Gary shitstorm coming her way.

"That's right," Everett said. "Nice to meet you, Michaela. I'll see you tomorrow, Sierra."

"Bye, Everett," she said.

She waited until the door shut before smiling at Michaela. "Give me twenty minutes to shower, and then we'll head to the market."

"Uh, hold the fuck up," Michaela said. "If you think we're not talking about Everett, you're crazy. Why did you kick him out?"

"I didn't kick him out," Sierra said.

"You so kicked him out. I could see it hurt his feelings, and I don't even know him," Michaela said. She tossed her long dark hair out of her face. "Is he a dick or something? Is that why you don't want us to hang out?"

"No, he's a great guy," Sierra said. "But Everett and I aren't exactly… we're not…."

Michaela held up her hand. "Your banging is casual. I get it."

Sierra grimaced. "I really hate this conversation."

Michaela laughed before putting her arm around her shoulders. "It could be worse. I could have walked in on the actual casual banging. It would have cost you a fortune in therapy bills."

"For you or for me?" Sierra asked.

Michaela laughed again. "Both. Go get in the shower."

Sierra hugged her. "I love you, honey. Thank you for driving here to check on me."

"Of course," she said. "I love you too, Mom."

CHAPTER 19

E verett grabbed water from the fridge and twisted off the bottle lid. He drank deeply before wiping his mouth and staring out the window above the sink.

It was Monday at noon, and Sierra was already gone when he'd arrived at her house this morning. He'd received a text from Sierra not long after that. She was out picking up paint and other supplies, but picking paint colours didn't take four hours.

She was avoiding him, and he hated how much that hurt. Almost as much as he'd hated the shame and panic on her face when her kid had walked in on them yesterday. It'd been more than apparent that Sierra didn't want Michaela to know she was involved with him. When the fuck would he stop being surprised by that? Sierra was perfectly fine with casual because she didn't want to date someone like him. Someone who would never fit into her world no matter how hard he tried.

The front door opened, and he took another quick drink of water to ease his suddenly dry throat and forced a smile on his face. He turned, the smile fading when he saw the goddamn mayor standing in the doorway.

He was shorter than Everett, with thinning grey hair and cold blue eyes. He looked Everett up and down and didn't try to hide the contempt in his gaze.

Everett met his look steadily. "Can I help you?"

The mayor's nostrils flared slightly. "Considering this isn't your house, no, you can't. Where is Sierra?"

"She's not here," Everett said.

Gary studied the drywall patches on the wall. "What happened there?"

"Is there a message you'd like me to pass on to Sierra?" Everett asked.

"You obviously don't know who I am," Gary said. "I'm -"

"I know who you are," Everett said.

Gary leaned against the doorway and folded his arms across his chest. "Do you always fuck your customers, Mr. Caine? That seems like bad business practice."

"Do you always stick your nose where it doesn't belong?" Everett asked.

"I think who Sierra is fucking is my business. She was my wife," Gary said.

"Was," Everett said. "Does your new wife know how invested you are in your ex-wife's personal life?"

A cold smile crossed Gary's face. "You know that Sierra is slumming with you, right? She's just fucking you to get free labour because she's sunk so much money into his ridiculous house, and she's almost broke. She would never sleep with someone like you otherwise."

"You don't know shit about Sierra," Everett said. "You never have."

"That's bullshit, and you know it. We were married for a long time, and I know her better than anyone. I know exactly what her type is, and you," Gary's gaze looked him up and down again, "are not it. She's using you, buddy. She wouldn't be caught dead in public with someone like you. She's a well-respected judge who isn't going to date a guy who's only a step above the people she convicts on a daily basis."

Everett fought like hell to keep his emotions from his face. But hearing Gary confirm everything Everett feared made him want to vomit. He'd known who Sierra was from the start, so why did Gary's words make Everett feel like his heart was being ripped out of his fucking chest?

He made himself smile at Gary. "I'll make sure to tell Sierra you stopped by."

"Stay away from my daughter. Sierra's life is already fucked, but my daughter has a bright future, and I don't want her associating with someone like you," Gary said before turning and leaving.

Everett waited until the front door shut before he slumped against the counter. He rubbed at his forehead, his stomach churning and bile coating the back of his throat.

SIERRA HEAVED THE PAINT CANS ON THE TABLE WITH A grunt. She'd picked up all the paint she needed for the basement. She was certain Everett would finish the basement today and wanted to get as much of the painting done this week as possible. She was back to work next week, and if she had the entire basement painted before then, she'd be well ahead of schedule.

She checked her watch. It was just after one, and she'd been gone much longer than she planned, but Indie had a rare weekday off and called to ask her if she wanted to have coffee. Coffee had turned into lunch, and despite her desire to talk to Everett about what happened yesterday, she'd sorely needed some girl time. She'd told Indie everything that happened, and getting it off her chest was a relief. She even felt a little more equipped to deal with Gary.

She pulled her phone from her purse and checked her messages. She'd expected furious texts and phone calls from Gary this morning. There was no way Michaela hadn't texted him last night to tell him about Everett, but she hadn't heard anything.

He was probably in meetings this morning, and she'd hear from him soon enough, but the waiting was killing her. Not that she wanted to listen to a fucking lecture from Gary about Everett, but it was better to get it over with.

She heard Everett's footsteps behind her and turned, giving him a tentative smile. "Hi there."

"Hello," he said. His gaze slipped to the paint cans on the table. "You got your paint."

"I did," she said.

"Must have been busy at the store," he said.

"Oh, no, Indie called and invited me for coffee, which turned into lunch," she said. "Sorry, I should have texted you."

He shrugged. "Why would you text me? We're not dating."

Shit. He was pissed about yesterday.

"I've finished the basement," he said. "I've packed up the truck and finished my cleanup, so I'll get the invoice sent to you tomorrow."

"Sounds good," she said. "Thank you for finishing it so quickly."

"You're welcome." A muscle ticked just below his right eye. "Gary stopped by this morning."

"Fuck." She leaned against the counter. "What did he say?"

"Nothing important," Everett said. "I've got to run. I'll see you around, Sierra."

"Everett, wait." She crossed the kitchen and caught his arm. "What did he say to you?"

"Nothing I didn't already know," he said.

"What's that supposed to mean?" she asked.

Frustration flickered across his face. "I have to go."

"You can give me five minutes," she said.

"Why? Because what I do isn't important? My time isn't as valuable as yours?"

"Whoa, where the fuck is this coming from?" she asked.

He sighed and raked his hand through his hair. "I think we should end things between us."

"Why?" she asked as her stomach immediately tried to evict her lunch salad.

"I just think it's time. What we've had has run its course," he said.

"Run its course? Are you fucking kidding me?" she said. "Look, I get that we're just casual, but that's a really dick thing to say to me."

He shoved his hands into his pockets. "How else should I say it?"

"You shouldn't say it at all," she said. "You've done nothing but run hot and cold with me throughout the whole relationship and -"

"It's not a relationship," he said.

"I know," she snapped. "I agreed to your stupid casual fucking thing even when I wanted more and -"

"You wanted more." Everett's laugh was bitter. "You're seriously going to try to feed me that line of bullshit, Sierra?"

"It's not bullshit," she said. "And I don't appreciate you

calling me a liar. I want more, Everett, but I also respect that you're not there yet. I was hoping that maybe with some time, we could -"

"Don't," Everett snarled. "Don't act like we could have a relationship when we both fucking know we can't."

"Why?" she said. "I get that you're busy with your job, but I'm busy with mine too. I'm not expecting you to spend every minute with me or -"

"You just can't admit it, can you?" Everett said.

"Admit what?" she asked.

"That you think I'm below you," Everett said. "You like to pretend that I'm your equal, but when push comes to shove, you don't want anyone knowing about your dirty little attraction to the drywaller."

"What in the actual fuck are you talking about?" Her temper exploded, and she put her fists on her hips, glaring at him. "I have never treated you like less or -"

"The one time we went out for dinner, you freaked out because we ran into a coworker. You couldn't spit it out fast enough that I was just your contractor. And yesterday with Michaela? I saw the look on your face when she walked in on us. You hated that she'd seen us together. Hated that your kid would see you slumming with someone like me."

"Everett, I -"

"Do you know why I said we should just be casual? It had nothing to do with my life and everything to do with yours. Because I knew who you were deep down, Sierra. I want more, but I deserve to be with someone who respects me," Everett said. "Who isn't ashamed to be seen with me. Who doesn't worry about what others say when they find out we're a couple. Who doesn't think they're better than me."

"Are you done?" she asked.

"We're done," he said.

He turned to leave, and she said, "Everett, stop. You got to say what you wanted. Now it's my fucking turn. You owe me that."

His body stiffened, but he turned and glared at her. "Fine."

"That judge we ran into at dinner? He's a misogynistic asshole who makes my life miserable at work. He also thinks he's friends with Gary, and if he'd suspected that you and I were dating, he would have immediately run to Gary with that information. I said what I said and acted how I did in an attempt to not deal with Gary riding my ass about sleeping with you."

She stalked back and forth in the kitchen. "And as much as I love my kid, she would - and did, obviously - go straight to Gary about you."

"You could have asked her not to," Everett said.

"It's not that easy," she said. "Asking her to keep a secret from Gary means popping that perfect family bubble I've worked so fucking hard to keep. It means hurting my kid and breaking my promise to her that we would always be a family."

She swallowed hard, her throat aching and tears stinging at her eyes. "I know that not being truthful with my kid or avoiding my ex-husband bitching at me about you makes me a selfish coward. I will own that selfish-ness, Everett. But I will not let you say it's because I think I'm better than you or ashamed to be seen with you. That couldn't be farther from the truth of how I feel about you."

Everett slumped against the doorway, regret all over his face. "Sierra, I'm sorry."

"Sorry for lying about your reasons for not dating me or believing I was a stuck-up snob?"

"Both," he said. "I shouldn't have lied or made that assumption."

"No, you shouldn't have," she said. "Do you know how much it hurts that you believe I'm that person?"

"I don't believe that," he said.

Her laugh was a little bitter. "Two minutes ago, you did."

"I'm sorry," he said. "Wendy, my ex, divorced me because she was ashamed of me. She even said she still loved me, but she couldn't be with someone like me anymore, not with her job and her friends and her colleagues. They expected better from her. I was no longer good enough."

She sighed. "I'm not your ex-wife."

"I know, and I hate that I let my past trauma affect our relationship. I swear if you give me a second chance, I'll do better," he said.

She wanted to say yes. She really fucking did. But her heart was lying in a battered mess at her feet, and dismissing or ignoring her hurt would do no good for either of them.

"I don't know if I can," she said. "Right now, I look at you, and all I see is a man who lied to me and couldn't see the real me even when I showed him who I was."

"I know," Everett said. "I'm sorry."

"I know you are," she said. "But I need some time."

The sorrow on Everett's face sent shards of glass through her heart. She hated hurting him but couldn't pretend to forgive and forget, no matter how much she loved him.

"Okay," he said. "You have my number."

"I do," she said.

He paused, his face pale as he studied her. "Goodbye, Sierra."

"Goodbye, Everett."

CHAPTER 20

"Michaela, you can stop worrying about me. I'm fine," Sierra said.

"Who said I'm worried about you?" Michaela asked.

Sierra sat on the couch and propped her feet on the coffee table. "You called me instead of texting. You never call."

"I wanted to hear your voice," Michaela said.

Sierra would have laughed if she wasn't so fucking miserable. "You just saw me this morning. Also, sweetie, I love you, but driving here every few days to say hello isn't necessary. You have your own life to live."

"Mom," Michaela was as stubborn as her, "I know you're sad. I know you miss Everett. Please tell me why you broke up."

"I told you - we didn't break up because we were never dating. It was a casual thing that," she swallowed hard, "ran its course."

"I don't believe you," Michaela said. "I think you really like this guy, and it's -"

She paused, and Sierra could hear Gary's voice in the

background before Michaela said, "I know, Dad. I'm ready to go. Just give me five minutes."

Sierra rubbed at her forehead as Michaela said, "I'm worried about you, Mom."

"I'm fine," Sierra lied. "I appreciate your concern, but you don't need to worry about me. I'm just tired from all the renovations, and the first week back to work was brutal."

"Why don't you come over to Dad and Roxanne's for dinner tonight," Michaela said. "You could use a little family time."

Sierra would rather drink hot wax. "Not tonight, sweetie. I have a headache, and I plan to take a long soak in the tub and go to bed early."

"That's not a fun Saturday night," Michaela said.

"I'm old," Sierra said, "It sounds like the perfect Saturday night to me."

"Mom, you - oh my God, yes, Dad. I'm coming," Michaela sighed with exasperation. "I gotta go. I told Dad I'd run some errands with him. I'll call you when we get back to see if you've changed your mind about dinner tonight."

She ended the call before Sierra could tell her not to bother. She tossed her phone on the couch and stared blankly at the ceiling. It'd been a week and a half since she'd last seen or talked to Everett, and the ache of missing him hadn't lessened as she'd hoped. It'd gotten worse if she was honest with herself, and she didn't know what the fuck to do about it.

She'd tried to stay busy with work and renovations and spending time with Indie and Hazel, but everything she did felt just a little bit wrong. Her appetite had nose-dived, and her enthusiasm for renovations had turned to dust. She'd painted one room in the basement before leaving it and putzing around with the renovation on what would be her home office.

She couldn't stand to be in the basement. It was beyond ridiculous, but she couldn't force herself to be down there. Hell, she could barely sleep in her own fucking bed. It felt too big, too empty, without Everett beside her.

So, call him. You miss him, and he was sincere in his apology. Why are you torturing us like this?

She stared at her phone sitting on the couch. As much as she missed him, she needed more time. Everett's belief that she was ashamed of him or thought she was better than him had hurt her badly. She'd spent a good portion of her life married to a man who looked down on others, and she had a healthy dose of shame for her complacent behaviour toward it. After leaving Gary, she'd vowed she'd never do something like that again nor allow another person's beliefs to over-shadow her own. To be accused of the very thing she'd hated most about Gary was a bitter pill to swallow.

Are you really going to give up the best thing that ever happened to you because he made an assumption? People make mistakes, Sierra.

She stood abruptly and headed upstairs. She would have her hot bath and maybe a glass or two or seven of whiskey and try to forget how much she missed Everett fucking Caine.

EVERETT STARED BLANKLY AT THE NEAT ROWS OF PACKAGED screws and nails in front of him. What the hell did he come to Home Depot for again? He scrubbed a hand across his beard. He had no fucking idea. Lately, he was lucky if he remembered to leave the house with his goddamn pants on.

It'd only been a week and a half since he'd ruined the best

thing that ever happened to him, but he felt like he'd aged twenty years. He was barely sleeping, had zero appetite, and his work was suffering. He was behind on his current job because he spent an embarrassing amount of time staring off into space, trying not to think about Sierra and failing miserably.

He reached for his phone before stopping himself. Sierra hadn't texted him, and checking his phone two hundred times a day wouldn't magically make a text appear. He didn't know how much time Sierra needed, but he wouldn't text her or call her, no matter how much he fucking missed her. He wouldn't be that guy, the one who didn't respect a woman when she asked for space. He'd hurt her so fucking badly, and he wouldn't do anything to make it worse.

Of course, it would be much easier to respect her request for time if he wasn't thinking about her, missing her, every minute of every fucking day.

He stared at the packages of screws and nails. Did he come here for nails? He couldn't fucking remember.

"Hello, Mr. Caine."

His body stiffened at the familiar voice, and he turned slowly, staring at Sierra's ex-husband. "Mayor Henson."

Gary shifted the shopping basket he held to his other hand. "My daughter tells me you've finished your contract work at Sierra's."

Everett didn't reply, and Gary said, "She also told me you and Sierra are no longer a 'thing'. I can't say that I'm surprised. I warned you that Sierra was only fucking you for some free renovations."

"Shut the fuck up," Everett said.

Everett had no doubt that Gary surrounded himself with 'yes men' and asskissers, and he took a perverse pleasure in the surprise that washed over Gary's face.

"There's no need to be rude, Mr. Caine," Gary said.

"Stop talking shit about Sierra," Everett said.

Gary laughed. "Impossible. Sierra is a terrible person and always has been. She's a stuck-up bitch who's only concerned with herself. She was a shitty wife and mother, and her self-ishness ruined the lives of everyone around her."

"That is such horseshit," Everett said. "Sierra is an incred-ible woman. She's intelligent and generous and an amazing mother. You spend so much time bringing her down because you know she's a better person than you'll ever be."

Gary laughed. "I see you're still drinking the Kool-Aid, even after she ended it. What exactly does she have over you, Mr. Caine? It can't be the sex. She was mediocre at best in bed."

Everett's hands clenched into fists, and he stalked toward Gary. He had no intention of hitting the man, but the look of fear that skittered across Gary's face was incredibly satisfy-ing. "You have no goddamn idea how lucky you were to have a woman like Sierra."

"She tore apart our family," Gary said. "She left me because she didn't want to be a mother because her career was more important to her than her child. Does that sound like the amazing woman you're making her out to be?"

"Do you even hear the lies you spew anymore?" Everett said. "She left you because you were a terrible husband who tried to control her. You couldn't stand how independent and strong she was, and now you punish her every way you can because she won't allow you to bully her."

"She left her child," Gary snarled. "She tore apart our family because she couldn't compromise, and it always had to be her way. She refused to put her child first."

"If that were true, she wouldn't still be putting up with your abuse. She puts Michaela first at every family dinner, every holiday spent with you, and every time she ignores the insults you throw at her whenever your kid isn't in the room. She lets Michaela believe that she's to blame for the divorce. She pretends it's no big deal when you try to turn Michaela against her. She puts aside her feelings because she wants Michaela to be happy and feel like she still has her family, even though you treat her like shit."

"She deserves it!" Gary snapped at him. "She should have just been a proper wife and did what I told her to do. It's her fault for thinking she was my equal."

"Do you even hear yourself?" Everett asked. "Whatever happened between the two of you, Sierra is the mother of your child and deserves respect."

"Sierra is a selfish whore who deserves to die alone," Gary spat.

"Dad!"

Gary's face turned white, and he gave Everett a sick look before turning slowly. Michaela stood behind him, her face even paler than his.

"Honey, I… you were going out to the car to call David, you said," Gary said.

"He was busy," Michaela said dully. "So, I came back to find you."

Gary swallowed hard. "What you just heard wasn't -"

"Stop it, Dad," she said. "Don't tell me more lies."

"I'm not," Gary said. "Mr. Caine, he goaded me into -"

"Stop lying to me!" Michaela shouted.

Gary winced and looked up and down the empty aisle. "Michaela, keep your voice down."

"Why? Because someone might hear the mayor's daughter yelling at him about what a shitty fucking person he is? God forbid your image is tarnished, right, Dad? Because that's all you care about, isn't it?" Tears slid down Michaela's face. "All this time, you've been... been torturing Mom behind my back."

"Don't be so dramatic, Michaela," Gary snapped with another look up and down the aisle, "and keep your voice down."

"No," Michaela said. "You don't get to tone police me or tell me how to feel about this, Dad. Not this fucking time."

Gary sucked in a deep breath and held out his hand. "Let's go, Michaela. We can discuss this in the car."

"Oh, I'm not going anywhere with you," Michaela said.

"Don't be ridiculous," Gary said. "You're going to take the bus home because of a misunderstanding?"

Michaela shook her head and skirted around him to stand next to Everett. "Everett, could you give me a ride?"

"No!" Gary snapped. "I forbid you to go anywhere with him, Michaela."

Michaela glared at him, looking so much like Sierra that Everett nearly did a double take. "I'm an adult, and you don't get to tell me what to do anymore."

She glanced at Everett. "Everett, can I hitch a ride?"

"Yes," he said.

"Thanks." She turned and marched down the aisle.

"It was good to see you again, Mr. Mayor," Everett said with a cold smile and walked away.

CHAPTER 21

"Mom!" The front door slammed, and the emotion in Michaela's voice made Sierra yank her robe over her damp body and hurry down the stairs.

"Mom, where are you?"

"Here. I'm here." Sierra ran into the living room. "Honey, what's wrong?"

She took one look at Michaela's face and immediately pulled her into her embrace. "Sweetie, what's going on? Is David okay?"

"He's fine," Michaela swiped at the tears on her cheeks.

"Your dad?" Sierra asked.

Michaela's face twisted. "Other than being an asshole, he's just fucking fine too."

Sierra blinked at her. She'd never heard Michaela speak that way about Gary before. She was a daddy's girl through and through. Sierra had no idea what Gary did to upset her, but she hated seeing Michaela so distraught.

She led Michaela to the couch, sitting beside her and taking her ice-cold hands. "Honey, I'm not sure what happened with your dad, but he's a good guy who loves you so much, and -"

"Don't, Mom." Michaela started to cry even harder. "Don't you lie to me too. Okay?"

Sierra smoothed the tears from Michaela's face with her thumbs. "Tell me what happened, honey."

Half an hour later, Michaela had told her everything, and they were both sitting at the kitchen table. Michaela's crying had turned to occasional watery hiccups, and she sipped at the green tea Sierra had made her.

"Why didn't you tell me what Dad said and did to you?" Michaela asked.

Sierra sighed. "Because I didn't want your relationship to be strained with him, honey. I know how much you love him, and he might have his flaws, but he loves you and is a good dad."

Michaela gave her a moody look. "But a terrible fucking husband."

"I wasn't always the best wife either," Sierra said.

"Stop, Mom," Michaela said. "You don't have to protect him anymore. I saw who he was, heard what he did to you straight from his own damn mouth. I'm done with him."

Feeling sick, Sierra took Michaela's hand before brushing her dark hair away from her tear-stained face. "I know you're angry with your dad right now, and you have every right to feel that way, but I want you to take some time to feel your emotions before you make any big decisions, okay? Again, your dad is far from perfect, but he loves you so much. How he feels about me doesn't change his feelings about you."

"I'm sorry, Mom," Michaela said. "I'm sorry I made you do all that stupid family shit with him and Roxanne."

"I'm not," Sierra said. "Was it difficult? Sometimes. But

seeing how happy you were made it all worth it. I promise you."

Michaela squeezed her hand. "You don't have to do it anymore, Mom, I promise."

They sat in silence for a few minutes. Michaela's phone buzzed, and she glanced at it before making a face. "Dad's called me, like, seventy-two times."

Sierra's phone rang, and she showed Michaela her screen. "Now he's calling me."

Michaela rolled her eyes, and Sierra smiled. "He's just worried about you, honey."

Michaela grabbed her phone and texted, her thumbs flying over the keyboard before she set it back on the table. "There. I told him I was fine but didn't want to talk to him right now. I said I was with the parent who didn't lie to me and to leave you the fuck alone too, or I'd never speak to him again."

Sierra winced, and Michaela shrugged. "He deserves it."

She gave Sierra an earnest look. "Everett is great, Mom."

"He is," Sierra said.

"The way he stuck up for you to Dad... it was crazy. He was like a damn white knight in the Home Depot aisle."

Sierra smiled. "I appreciate that he came to my defense."

"You're going to call him, right?" Michaela said. "I don't know what he did to you, but defending you to Dad has to win him some points."

"How do you know he did anything to me?" Sierra said. "Maybe I was the asshole."

Michaela shook her head. "I know you weren't. When he dropped me off here, I asked Everett to come inside, and he said he couldn't. He said he'd hurt you, and you didn't want to see him right now."

Sierra stared at her green tea as Michaela said, "You don't have to tell me what he did, but was it similar to what Dad did?"

"No," Sierra said. "Honestly, it wasn't that bad. But it hurt my feelings a whole lot, and I was worried he would never see the real me, just the person he'd decided I was."

"I don't think that's true," Michaela said. "What he said to Dad about you was spot on. He knows exactly who you are. Also, how he looked when he told me he hurt you... I think he might be in love with you, Mom."

Sierra swallowed hard, her voice hoarse when she said, "I think I might be in love with him too."

"Shit," Michaela said. "You need to go to him right now and tell him that."

"This isn't a romantic movie," Sierra said. "I can't just bang on his door and blurt out that I love him."

"Sure you can," Michaela said.

"I don't even know where he lives," Sierra said.

"You could text him and ask him to come here, but that won't have the same emotional impact as a surprise 'I love you' visit."

"Michaela, I can't -"

"Wait, you said he was friends with Hendrix, right?" Michaela grabbed her phone and started texting.

"What are you doing?" Sierra asked.

"I'm texting Hazel. I told her you're in love with Everett, and she needs to ask Hendrix for Everett's address so you can go over there and confess your love."

"Oh my God, Michaela, Hazel's at work and Saturday's are busy. She won't -"

Michaela's phone dinged, and she made an excited yelp. "She just sent me the address! Oh, and she says, and I quote, 'Go get your man, you gorgeous bitch'."

She laughed delightedly and stood, pulling Sierra to her feet. "Go put on something sexy and put a little makeup on, for heaven's sake. I'll send you Everett's address."

"Michaela, I can't -"

"Mom." Michaela's hands cupped her face, and she stared directly at her. "Do you love this man?"

"Yes," Sierra said.

"Then tell him. You can't wait for happiness to find you. You have to chase it."

Sierra stared at her before a grin broke out across her face. "When did you get so much smarter than me, honey?"

Michaela grinned and gave her a loud smacking kiss on the lips. "You'll always be more brilliant than me. Now, go get your man. Also, maybe snap some pics for me so I can Instagram this love story."

"I love you, sweetie, but no fucking way to the Instagram," Sierra said.

Michaela laughed and pushed her toward the stairs. "Fair enough."

SIERRA COULDN'T REMEMBER THE LAST TIME SHE'D BEEN THIS nervous. She smoothed her dress and ran her tongue over her front teeth, hoping like hell she didn't have any traces of lipstick on them.

She stood on the front step of Everett's modest bungalow, staring at the doorbell like it might bite her if she touched it. Everett's work truck was in the driveway, so she knew he was home, but she couldn't work up the courage to ring the doorbell.

"C'mon, woman, just fucking do it," she muttered.

"Sierra?"

She whirled around, nearly falling off the step, and stared at Everett. He stood on the sidewalk behind her, holding the leash of a small, fluffy white dog.

"You have a dog," she said.

He glanced at the dog. "No, I walk Misty when Jean's arthritis is bad."

"Jean?" she said.

"My neighbour." Everett glanced at the bungalow to the right of his. As if she'd heard them, the door opened, and an older woman with long white hair and a cane in one hand hobbled out onto the front step.

Misty barked excitedly and danced at Everett's feet. He bent and scooped her up, carrying her to Jean. He set Misty inside, and Jean closed the door before patting Everett's cheek with one vein-ladled hand. "Thank you, Everett. You're a good boy to help an old woman and her dog."

"You're welcome, Jean," Everett said. "Don't forget that tomorrow is garbage day. I'll come by later this evening to gather your garbage and take it to the curb, okay?"

"Thank you, dearest," Jean said, patting his cheek again. "I'll make you some cookies to thank you. Do you want chocolate chip or oatmeal raisin?"

"Oatmeal raisin," he said with a small smile.

"I'll make them tomorrow," Jean said and shuffled back into her house. Everett waited until she'd closed the front door before joining Sierra. "Come in."

She followed him into the house, smoothing her dress again as she followed him to his small but efficient looking kitchen. He tossed his keys on the table. "Do you want a beer?"

"No," she said. "Everett -"

"How is Michaela?" he asked. "She was pretty upset when I dropped her off."

"She's feeling better. Pissed at her dad, and I don't think her relationship with Gary will ever be the same, but that's on him," Sierra said.

"I'm glad she's feeling better," Everett said.

"Everett, I -"

"I love you, Sierra." Everett looked both scared to death and determined as hell. "I know it's shitty timing to tell you that, but I needed you to know how I feel, even if you're here to tell me you never want to see me again."

"Oh man, Michaela's gonna be pissed at you," Sierra said.

Everett stared at her in confusion. "What? Why?"

"Because she sent me here to tell you I loved you in a big 'romantic movie' reveal, but you beat me to it."

"You love me," Everett said.

"So fucking much," Sierra said. "I love you, Everett Caine."

Giddiness with a healthy dose of relief washed over his face. "I love you, Sierra Lewis."

"Of course you do," she said. "I'm awesome."

He laughed and breached the distance between them with two large strides. He wrapped his arms around Sierra and lifted her, kissing her hard as she cupped his face. When he released her, she said, "Now, that was a fucking romantic movie moment."

He laughed again and hugged her. "Sierra, I'm so fucking sorry for what I said and what I thought about you. I was an idiot, and I promise I see the real you."

"I know," she said. "Michaela told me exactly what you said to Gary. Thank you for having my back, honey."

"I will always have your back, sweetheart," he said. "You're amazing, and I promise I will never forget that."

She kissed his throat. "I love you, and I'm proud of who you are. You know that, right?"

"Yes," he said. "I love you too."

"Good. Now, why don't you take me upstairs and show me how much you love me with a spanking and multiple orgasms," she said.

He grinned. "Whatever you want, Judge Lewis."

EPILOGUE

"You don't dance. Ever?" Everett leaned closer to Sierra so he could hear her over the music.

"Ever," she said. "I look like a baby giraffe learning to walk when I dance. It's not sexy at all."

"She's not that bad," Hazel said. She sat across the table from them, a glass of wine in one hand. "I saw her dance once, and there was a bit of mild flailing, but it was cute."

"It was absolutely not cute," Sierra said.

There was a cheer from the dance floor, and they turned to look. A crowd had gathered around Indie and Val. Looking gorgeous in her wedding gown, Indie was staring at her new husband with shock and delight.

Beyonce's *Single Lady* was blasting, and Val, his daughter Raven, Hazel's son Spencer, and Michaela were doing a perfect rendition of the song's choreography.

"Holy shit," Hendrix joined them, handing Sierra a glass of whiskey as he sat beside Hazel. He sipped at his beer. "Did you know Spencer could dance like that?"

"Yes," Hazel said with a laugh. "Spence and Michaela spent an entire summer together perfecting this routine as kids. I didn't, however, have any idea that Val also knew the choreography."

"Damn, he's light on his feet for a big guy," Everett said.

"I can't look away," Hendrix said. "Is it weird that I'm kind of attracted to Val right now?"

"You and me both, brother." Everett clinked his beer bottle against Hendrix's as Sierra laughed.

"As cute as your newfound attraction to Val is, I'm pretty sure Indie will want him to spend their wedding night with her."

"Hey," Hendrix wiggled his ring finger at her, showing off the silver wedding band that adorned it, "I can't act on the attraction anyway. I'm a married man now, remember?"

"I do," Sierra said. "Probably because I was the one who caught you when you nearly fainted at the altar."

"It was very warm," Hendrix said, "and I was nervous. Also, Hazel's beauty is enough to bring a man to his knees."

"Smooth, honey," Hazel said with a grin. "Very smooth."

"Thank you," Hendrix said. "Now, if I could only get Preston to stop sending me the video every day of me nearly fainting at the altar, I'd be golden."

Hazel laughed. "He sends it to me too."

"Oh God," Hendrix said. "I will never live this down."

"It's only been a year since it happened," Hazel said. "He'll stop eventually."

"Will he, though?" Hendrix said sadly.

The three of them laughed, and Hendrix grinned at Hazel before kissing her.

"So," Everett said to Sierra, "back to this no dancing thing. I assume this means we won't be having a dance at our wedding?"

"Oh, we'll have one. Just don't expect me to dance," Sierra said.

Everett picked up her hand, kissing her knuckle above her engagement ring. "Not even one dance? We have to have a first dance, right?"

"I mean, it's not like a rule or anything."

"I think it might be," Everett said. He leaned closer, pressing his mouth against her ear so only she could hear him. "You know what happens when you break the rules, sweetheart."

He felt her little shiver of delight against him, and he rubbed her thigh under the table. "If you promise you'll dance with me once at our wedding, I'll reward you with a spanking and a very thorough pussy eating later tonight."

Another shiver of anticipation, and she gave him that sassy, perfect grin he loved. "I promise, Everett Caine."

ABOUT THE AUTHOR

Elizabeth Kelly was born and raised in Ontario, Canada. She moved west as a teenager and now lives in Alberta with her husband and a menagerie of pets. She firmly believes that a person can survive solely on sushi and coffee, and only her husband's mad cooking skills prevents her from proving that theory.

For more information about Elizabeth, check out her website at

www.elizabethkelly.ca

facebook.com/EKellyBooks

twitter.com/ElizabethKBooks

instagram.com/elizabethkelly_author

amazon.com/Elizabeth-Kelly/e/B00EOHZ0MS

bookbub.com/authors/elizabeth-kelly

ALSO BY ELIZABETH KELLY

Tempted Series

Tempted

Twice Tempted

Forever Tempted

Breathless

Tempted Trilogy (Books 1-3)

Red Moon Series

Red Moon

Red Moon Rising

Dark Moon

Alpha Moon

Pale Moon

The Recruit Series

The Recruit (Book One)

The Recruit (Book Two)

The Recruit (Book Three)

The Recruit (Book Four)

The Recruit (Book Five)

The Recruit (Book Six)

The Shifters Series

Willow and the Wolf (Book One)

Ava and the Bear (Book Two)

Katarina and the Bird (Book Three)

Porter's Mate (Book Four)

Bria and the Tiger (Book Five)

Rosalie Undone (Book Six)

The Dragon's Mate (Book Seven)

Rise of the Jaguar (Book Eight)

The Assassin and the Bear (Book Nine)

The Draax Series

Reign (Book One)

Rule (Book Two)

Rebel (Book Three)

Surrender (Book Four)

Harmony Falls Series

Sweet Harmony (Book One)

Perfect Harmony (Book Two)

Forbidden Harmony (Book Three)

Redeeming Harmony (Book Four)

Absolute Harmony (Novella)

Beautiful Harmony (Book Five)

Seasoned Romance Series

Bet Your Heart on Me (Book One)

Take a Chance on Me (Book Two)

Place Your Trust in Me (Book Three)

Individual Books

The Necessary Engagement

Amelia's Touch

The Rancher's Daughter

Healing Gabriel

The Contract

A Home for Lily

Saving Charlotte

Shameless

The Fairy Tales Collection

Broken

An Unlikely Seduction

Holiday Romance

The Christmas Wife

The Christmas Rescue

The Christmas Nanny

The Christmas Boss

Sordid Games